To FIRE,
It has been some
time. Hope this is
worth the wait.
See you at Mid-
Night!.

Terry B.

8-19-2007

nHouse

Here's what some book club reviewers had to say about **Dancer's Paradise: An Erotic Journey,** part one of the *Dancer's Paradise* trilogy:

"…The author is a talented writer with a niche in a subject that's not overly saturated by African American authors. I do look forward to other works from this author in the future. If you like EROTIC LITERATURE, Paradise awaits…"

—T. Rhythm Knight, APOOO Book Club

"A SENSUAL story of FRIENDSHIP…Debrena struggles with issues of IDENTITY and SEXUALITY…I found it to be…full of HUMAN EMOTIONS."

—Dawn, Mahogany Book Club

"…This was a truly AMAZING novel and the STORYLINE FLOWED from one chapter to the next without missing a beat…"

—Pamela Bolden, The RAWSISTAZ Reviewers

"…A POWERFUL STORY of one woman's journey into her own sexuality. Terry B. brings insight into the choices often associated with RELATIONSHIP, IDENTITY and LOVE…"

—Samantha Jiles, A Nu Twist A Flavah Reviewer

"…Dancer's Paradise takes you through trials, tribulations, and triumphs as Debrena Allen takes us on A RIDE OF SELF-DISCOVERY…"

—Valencia, FIRE Book Club

"…Dancer's Paradise is an EROTIC THRILL RIDE that crosses all boundaries of SEXUAL IDENTITY and explores the human spirit…explores heavily forbidden situations that are as intense as those depicted in the movie *She Hate Me* by Spike Lee…the flip side to J. L. King's *On The Down Low*…a DARING book and worthy of reading…CLEVER and ORIGINAL…"

—A YOUnity Guild Book Club

AT MIDNIGHT

TERRY B.
is the penname for Terry W. Benjamin
and Tobias A. Fox

Also by Tobias A. Fox
and Terry W. Benjamin
written under their penname Terry B.:

Fiction
Dancer's Paradise: An Erotic Journey

Memoirs
Also by Keith Lynch
with (Tobias A. Fox using the penname) Terry B.:
Dirty Justice: Who Killed Mommy

AT MIDNIGHT

Choice Fowler's Story

TERRY B.

nHouse Publishing, L.L.C.

Newark

This is a work of fiction. Names, characters, places, and incidents either are the product of the author's imagination or are used fictitiously, and any resemblance to actual persons, living or dead, business establishments, events, or locales is entirely coincidental.

nHouse

nHouse Publishing, L.L.C.
P.O. Box 1038
Newark, New Jersey 07101
973-223-9135
www.nhousepublishing.com

At Midnight
ISBN   13-digit 978-0-9726242-0-6
ISBN   10-digit 0-9726242-0-1
Library of Congress Catalog Number 2006909557
Women, Hip-Hop, African American, Multicultural, Contemporary, Gay & Lesbian – Fiction

Cover design and layout by Asen James
Book design by About Faces Graphics
Edited by Marcela Landres

Printed in Canada

I knew any thought of us getting back together was crazy. Yet I had fantasized that somehow, someway, we'd get back together. That by some miracle, things would work out for us. A way to make whole the love that fell apart so abruptly; of course there were no way things could be worked out after I discovered that Debrena Allen was into women.

—Choice Fowler

AT MIDNIGHT

PROLOGUE

CHOICE

1982

The day started like any other day in our two-story house that my father built from the ground up. This was done with the help of his friends in the artistic community that he established in a remote part of L.A.—an area that many Hollywood celebrities called home until the earthquake of 1980. After that, my father and his friends were able to buy all the land they wanted.

That morning, after he fixed me breakfast, we went to work. Stretching canvasses over frames he made the night before, we worked in silence, but it wasn't companionable as it usually was. I tried hard to draw him into a conversation, but he was too distracted and beneath the distraction was an anger that I'd never seen before.

I tried to talk to him, but I realized that nothing I could say would make him feel better.

They called my father Lucky and my mother Queen, and so did I at my father's request. They were the most admired couple amongst neighbors and friends. They were royalty in the artistic community. But the truth of the matter was that the kingdom had been shaken and fallen and no one knew how to put it back together again.

Lucky had told me that everything would be all right, and although I wanted to believe him, I knew better. It was such a strange feeling that I actually became sick. Although we had no kind of health insurance, Lucky got one of his friends to take me to the emergency room. The doctor explained to Lucky that I had experienced an anxiety attack, and that I would be all right if I took the Valium that he prescribed for me. Lucky took me home, but never got me the Valium. His thought was that we needed more father and son talks. I was suffering because of what was going on between him and Queen.

That day, Lucky made me grilled cheese for lunch. I asked him to eat with me, but he said he wasn't hungry which puzzled me because I hadn't seen him eat anything in the past two days. He sat with me for a little while, then suddenly rose from the table like he had remembered there was something that he needed to do. After I finished my lunch I washed the dishes, and then went looking for him. I found him in the bedroom he shared with Queen.

"Lucky," I called out to him. "She's not coming back."

"We don't know that, son."

I frowned. He was standing in the bedroom surrounded by white boxes that Queen had gotten together to pack up most of her things.

"I said I wasn't going to do this. I don't want to put you back in the hospital. I promised myself to be straight with you, son."

I was very glad to hear him say that, but I must admit I didn't understand.

"Queen and I…," Lucky began, then stopped. "You're just…too…young…to be going through this."

I looked at Lucky, my father, my hero.

"I told you that everything would be all right."

He looked like a man that had lost something precious.

"I want to fix everything, son. So that you will never have to live like I had to live. In a situation where I didn't know what would happen from one day to the next. I want you to have the security of a family that I never had. But this is something I just can't fix by myself."

"Queen's not coming back," I said. I hadn't heard anything from her in over a week.

"It's not that simple, son. I..we…"

Lucky stopped talking when he saw the tears collect in my eyes.

"I could call her sometimes," I said tentatively. "And maybe she could come here…or I could…go where she is. And we could be together, for a little while, and then I could come back to you."

"If I could just fix this thing," Lucky said, so much pain in his voice that I had to turn away from him. That was when the tears began to slide down my face. "I could humble myself; let her know that whatever she has done could be forgiven. That we could put it behind us and move on." At ten years old I can't say that I totally understood what Lucky was telling me, but I knew that he was struggling with the biggest burden of his life and it was beating him down. But I also felt that he could never let it bring him down to the point where he couldn't get up from under it. I always saw my father as a warrior.

"Move on and be family," Lucky said.

It was something he wanted for me and Queen. A family where the mother and father sleep in the same bed and the son would find them there in the morning, and could feel free to climb up into the bed and lay between them and feel warm and secure.

That's all that I ever wanted.

"It's gonna be all right, son. It's gonna be all right. If me and Queen could talk to each other. Everything would be all right."

I turned to my father with hope. "Why can't y'all just talk?"

Lucky smiled, but there was sadness in his eyes. "I wish it was that simple. Because we haven't been talking, things have gotten out of hand."

"You can call Auntie Jenna," I suggested. "She'll let you speak to Queen."

"I think someday soon we will talk. The time just isn't right, son."

"But when y'all talk, then everything will be all right?"

"Yes, I believe it will."

I wanted to believe Lucky. But it was so hard with Queen

away for so long. Even when I heard her voice on the phone, she seemed so far away. She told me she was staying with Auntie Jenna. Auntie Jenna wasn't my real aunt, no blood relation to me, but she was my mother's best friend. They were like sisters since before I was born.

My father reached out and pulled me into his hard body. My head rested on his stomach as he held me tight.

Queen walked into the room.

Even though I was facing away from the doorway, I knew the distinctive slap of her bare feet on the hardwood floors.

"How's my little man?" Queen asked as I turned toward her. She was dressed in one of the outfits that Auntie Jenna had designed for her: a loose linen top with matching wide legged pants. Even though she wasn't a professional, Queen was the model for Auntie Jenna's catalog of original designs for petite women. Auntie Jenna would often say that Queen was the "petitest of the petite," and then she would laugh and Queen would frown like being small was something that she didn't want to be reminded of.

"It's like I live in a land of giants," Queen once told me. "I'm glad you're tall, Choice. You take after Lucky. People don't always take you serious when you're small like me."

Lucky was big in comparison, just six feet, well shaped and muscular with dreadlocked hair that he wore like a lion's mane. People would stop them on the street and tell them what a beautiful couple they made.

Two beautiful people that just couldn't get it together, I thought.

"Choice, baby, I need to talk to Lucky," Queen said.

I smiled, then pressed my face into Lucky's slim torso. I used his dark tee shirt to wipe away my tears. "Talk is the best thing, right Lucky?" I asked.

Lucky smiled.

"You said if you two could talk everything would be all right," I reminded him.

Lucky said nothing, just kept on smiling as he patted my back.

"I'll leave you two alone so that y'all can talk."

I got a big hug from Queen before I left the room.

I walked upstairs and found myself in the wide room where Lucky kept his turntables, big black speakers, and an album collection so extensive that it nearly reached the ceiling. Lucky loved his R&B and he played it all the time, especially artists like Al Green, Teddy Pendergrass, and Rick James, and groups like the Delfonics, the Dramatics, the Spinners, the Stylistics, and Blue Magic.

I always got a kick out of seeing Lucky handle his music. He would pull an album from the tightly packed shelves, slide the black vinyl record out, and gently put it on the turn table. Then he would put the specially ordered diamond needle on the record and stand back, like he was in awe.

"I may not be able to play an instrument," Lucky once told me, "but I can play me some music."

I had to ask for permission if I ever wanted to listen to his music. He would always let me listen in his presence to make sure I didn't scratch any of his records and that I rubbed the record clean with his special cloth once I was finished.

Then I heard Queen scream.

There was a loud gunshot that made me cover my ears and fall back hard against the wall. At the second gunshot I slid down the wall, with my hands pressed to my ears. By the third gunshot, I was screaming and crying.

CHAPTER 1

I t was the summer of 2000.

They were two among a crowd in the loft. They were whispering, but because I was listening so hard I heard every word. They were at an invitation only event, admiring photos by me, Choice Fowler. A man and a woman talked like they were at home alone. They were well groomed and expensively dressed like all the others floating around them. Everyone was expected to dig deep into their fat pockets and buy something at this summer showcase. According to Carrie Nelson, the founder and CEO of the Nelson Talent Agency, I was "the next big thing in Black photography, the Black man rising."

They stood with their backs toward me, not even realizing I was breathing down their necks, listening.

"She seems to be in another place," the woman whispered, her voice soft and silky smooth.

"Like she's dancing, but it's more than that," the man said, in a hard baritone with a touch of bass. "More like sex."

The woman put her hand up to her mouth and giggled as she moved closer to the man. "You can't have sex on the dance floor."

"Why not?"

"I know you have to be joking. Because what you're saying, what you're suggesting is just too crazy," the woman said. "We've done some wild things."

"But not that. Not yet."

The woman giggled, and moved even closer to the man. "You need to see somebody, somebody professional. You must be some kind of sex addict."

The man moved in closer to the picture. "She seems to be at peace."

That shot was a gift from the gods. It wasn't planned, but it was perfect, nothing I could get from a model posing for me. I had come upon her dancing alone in the studio. I wasn't supposed to be there, but I was glad that I was. I called the photo *Dancer's Paradise*. It was a picture of Debrena Allen, a former lover, a featured dancer with the Dominique St. Claire Dance Studio.

I knew any thought of us getting back together was crazy. Yet I had fantasized that somehow, someway, we would. Of course there was no way things could be worked out after I discovered that Debrena was into women. I hated that scene; I just couldn't understand what that was about. I once read somewhere that the most popular male fantasy was sex with two women at the same time. What was the biggest sexual fantasy for women? I couldn't find any research in that area, but I had known women, on both the West Coast and the East Coast, who swung like that. Maybe I'm a little strange, but watching two women together or sharing a bed with two women was not a turn on for me, especially if I had some respect and love for one of the women involved.

A hand rested on my shoulder.

"You have to mix and mingle, Brother Man," Curtis Walker said as he stood beside me, dressed in a white linen suit. His custom made shirt was two-tone, blue and black, and he wore a bowtie in the stiff collar. On his feet were silk socks and ridiculously expensive Stacey Adams shoes. He was a pretty boy fashion plate. I tried hard not to like him, but he was funny, and he worked hard at NTA as a talent scout.

"You're doing enough mixing and mingling for both of us," I said, noticing that he had a glass of wine in one hand and a plate of chopped cheese and whole wheat crackers in the other. I didn't expect him to spend too much time with me because he was working the room.

"It's my job," Curtis said.

"And I can't thank you enough."

"You'll thank me, and Carrie, and Dany when this show ends and the big bucks start rolling in," Curtis said. "Lucky for you, a lot of people like to look at beautifully shot photographs."

"There are a lot of voyeurs in here," I observed, lowering my voice. The sexy whisperers seemed rooted to the space in front of Debrena's photo.

"I like to watch," Curtis admitted. From our many drunken conversations he let me know that watching two women together was at the top of his sexual fantasy wish list.

"Sometimes watching is a lot safer than getting involved." A year had past since the summer I met Debrena and I was still trying to get over her.

"That photo is going to bring in some big bucks," Curtis said "And to think, you didn't want to include that in your show."

I couldn't explain that by exhibiting Debrena's photo, I was labeling myself as a lovesick fool. I didn't want to go out like that. No one likes to be assed out in public. All the classic R&B songs talked about lost love, but what they didn't tell you was how long the hurt would last, nor how hard it would make a man cry.

How could I move on in the summer of 2000 when my mind, body, and spirit had been crushed in the summer of 1999? I had to admit to myself that I was madly in love with Debrena Allen.

CHAPTER 2

I felt a little shabby standing next to Curtis in his fancy clothes, and me in my white and burgundy trimmed track suit.

"Are those your formal sweats?" Curtis asked.

"Like I always tell you, Curtis, it's not about me being a fashion plate, it's about the models. Besides, you've seen me work; I'm all over the floor. A fancy suit wouldn't stand a chance with me."

"Do you even own a suit?"

"One black suit," I admitted. "For funerals and weddings."

Curtis laughed. "I got to take you shopping, to make Miss Carrie happy if nothing else."

"Don't do me any favors."

Curtis laughed again. "I'm doing it more for me, Brother Man. I'm about to make some serious moves and I need Miss Carrie on my side. With your sweats—"

"Track suits."

"Whatever. With your track suits, and muscle shirts, and khakis, and leather running shoes, you look like a professional athlete relaxing around his million-dollar home.

"What's wrong with that? I'm neat and clean and well covered."

"You're not a jock, Brother Man," Curtis said in a harsh whisper. "You're an artist. But you also need to be a businessman."

"And dress like you?"

Curtis smiled, "I'm about art and business, and that's not a bad combination. You should take notes."

"I got to be me, Curtis."

Curtis shook his head. "You're almost hopeless."

"You're saying I have nothing going for myself?"

"I can't say that. You're a bad man with that camera and a wizard in the darkroom. Can't nobody touch you when it comes to that. You can walk up to any honey on the street and talk her into posing naked for you."

"And you're impressed with that." Curtis Walker called my nude studies "*nekkid* pictures" and loved to hang out in the loft to check out who I had "talked out of their panties."

"Hey, man, call me shallow," Curtis admitted. "But I got to wine and dine a honey before she even thinks about taking her clothes off."

"I always tell you, Curtis. It's all about art."

"A naked woman is a naked woman, whether she is in a museum or in *Black Tail* magazine."

Dany Nelson came over with a worried look on her face. I wasn't too concerned because she always wore that look. When it came to business, and selling my work *was* her business, she was a no nonsense woman. That afternoon she was the voice of gloom and doom. "Things couldn't be worse," she said instead of hello.

"You got to get some big ballers up in this piece," Curtis told Dany. "Some shot callers. These folks are here for show. They are here to see and be seen. They'd break all of the Ten Commandments before they'd break a bill."

"Not so loud," Dany whispered. "We have a few more hours."

"You are the eternal optimist," Curtis told Dany.

Dany wore a dark summer weight coat dress and stacked heels. At five-nine, and a size six, she stood out in any crowd. Her one flaw was her black rimmed, over sized eyeglasses. Curtis was always telling her that she needed to wear contact lenses like he did.

"This is business," Dany told Curtis. "I know my business. I just wish Choice would help me more."

"I'm here, Dany. I'm minding the store."

"You have to mingle, Choice. They know your work, but they don't know you. Nobody knows you."

"You want me to work the room like I'm running for some type of office. I can't do that. I'm not comfortable with that."

Dany's dark eyes cut me from behind her eyeglasses. "I don't know why I bust my ass for you."

"Because I'm cute?"

Dany smiled. "You're cute all right, but you'd be cuter if you'd help me sell some of your work."

"I'll do what I can."

"You know it would help if you'd let me sell *Dancer's Paradise*. There's a lot of interest in that photo."

"We had this discussion. I told you and Curtis that I didn't want that shot in this show. You not only ignored my request, you put that shot on the cover of the invitations."

"It worked," Dany quickly added. "This is not a bad crowd."

"Just a cheap crowd," Curtis added.

Dany looked at him like she wanted to punch his lights out. "Like I said, we have a little more time here today."

"Well, it was nice talking to you guys," Dany said, "but I got to jump back into the arena. You'll come out of this with some money, Choice Fowler. You'll get paid, and so will NTA; we've got too much invested in you to leave you to your own devices."

"I want to help," I blurted out before Dany left to continue her mixing and mingling. She stood still. "I'll move around a little, let these people know who I am."

Dany put her hands together in the prayer position. "Thank you, Choice Fowler, the magnificent."

"I can do without sarcasm," I told her, but I was smiling. "You know I have to leave for L.A. by the end of this week."

"I know; that's why I rushed to put this together."

"Let's do this then, and let's get that other thing together. I talked to your mother, and she really wants it to happen."

"I know that, Choice," Dany said, somewhat defensively. "I

know what kind of team you need to start that project."

"I just want to do the best job for NTA. I have my stylist, I have my hair person, but I can't really make it happen without a makeup artist."

"I know that, Choice," Dany said with her eyes darting around the room. "I plan to have some people for you to look at before you leave for vacation."

With that, Dany disappeared into the crowd.

CHAPTER 3

Lorrie

Angela King and Marcy Chase stood before Reverend Jackie Brown, looking absolutely beautiful. They both had their hair done at Karen Jackson's beauty salon. Marcy wore a white mini-dress with lacey panels and ankle tie sandals. On her fingers were white crotched fingerless gloves. Angela wore a black, man's style tuxedo with black lapels and a pinched waist. On her feet were black patent leather pumps.

They stood before Reverend Brown as she raised her hands, her long black robe completely covering her voluptuous frame. "Good afternoon, everyone," she said, silver rings on each of her fingers, smiling so broadly it became contagious; we all smiled along with her. "It is a great pleasure to welcome you all to witness such a special occasion. Today we celebrate the love between Angela and Marcy."

I looked around for Debrena and found her standing near the entrance to the kitchen. She looked extra special in a green embroidered tank top and a rust colored chiffon mini-skirt.

"At this time I have two questions for those gathered here, and hopefully you will answer 'We will' as I ask them," Reverend Brown went on.

I felt queasiness in the pit of my stomach because I disliked all forms of audience participation. I hated when performers asked concert goers to sing along, or wave their hands in the air, or yell or scream like idiots. I felt like I was doing their work for them; I had come to be entertained, not to be a part of the performance.

Reverend Brown asked, "Will you support Angela and Marcy as a loving couple and growing individuals?" and "Will you support them in their trials and tribulations, rejoice in their happiness, and lovingly remind them of the vows they will make to each other on this great afternoon?"

Everyone present said, "We will" to both questions.

Then there were the exchange of vows. Under the direction of Reverend Brown, Angela was the first: "I, Angela King, take you, Marcy Chase, as my partner for life." Marcy repeated the same words, and then they exchanged rainbow rings. After that, two gay men sang two songs a cappella, Anita Baker's "Giving You The Best That I Got" and Luther Vandross's "Here and Now."

The commitment ceremony wrapped up with Angela and Marcy lighting candles, another symbol of their union. After they kissed and Reverend Brown's final blessing, they led everyone out of the house and onto the sundeck.

I hung back because I didn't want to get smashed by the crowd, and I also wanted to say something to Debrena. I found her deep in the kitchen, alone. She was standing with her face in her hands, weeping so hard that her shoulders shook. I was shocked because I had never known Debrena to be emotional, and I had known her since we were both ten years old.

"D," I tentatively called out, "you all right?"

She walked forward and hugged me so tightly that I found it hard to breathe. Even though it hurt I held onto her.

"I didn't want anyone to see me like this," Debrena admitted, wiping her face with her hands and smudging her makeup in the process.

"I understand," I said, although I didn't. I looked around the kitchen and found some napkins. I handed them to her and she used them to dry her face.

"I don't want you to think I'm a softie," Debrena told me around a crooked smile. "It's just that I can't believe how strong their love is. I feel like Angela is ready to do anything to make Marcy happy."

I was stunned when the tears began to flow again. I handed Debrena another wad of napkins.

"This is getting ridiculous," Debrena said. "But Angela is so 'there' for Marcy. When Marcy approached me about using my house for their commitment ceremony, I thought it was about Marcy wanting this. But Angela is 'there', Lorrie. Angela is so 'there' for Marcy. Would you be willing to go all out for me like that?"

"Yes," I said without hesitation.

Debrena looked at me distrustfully. It made me think of that night a few months ago when Angela and Marcy were hanging out with me and Debrena in Debrena's house. I could never be sure if it happened because we all had been drinking Bacardi and Coke, or if it was something that Marcy needed to do to prove her love for Angela.

We were playing *Truth or Dare,* like we had seen in that Madonna movie and Angela dared Marcy to walk around the block in her underwear. It was evening, but there was still a lot of light outside.

Marcy did it.

We all gathered on the front porch as Marcy came out of the house, barefoot and in her thong panties and an almost nothing bra. There were neighbors on their porches and there were cars on the street blowing their horns, but there was no turning back for Marcy. She disappeared around the block, and it had to be a good ten minutes before we saw half naked Marcy again.

Her face was tight as she walked toward us, like a soldier on a mission. Angela stepped off the porch and met Marcy in the middle of the block. They embraced, and then kissed. When they stepped up onto the porch, it was Angela who was in tears.

"How far would you go for me?" Debrena asked as we stood in her kitchen.

"Whatever you want me to do, I will do," I said.

I wanted to prove my commitment, my devotion, my love to Debrena. I wanted her to test me like Angela tested Marcy.

CHAPTER 4

"Y ou don't want to dance anymore?" Debrena asked as we lay naked in her bed.

I looked up at the ceiling, trying to regain control of my emotions. We had just made love and began talking since neither one of us could go to sleep. This was odd because usually after we made sweet love, sleep came to take both of us. I think it was because she was going on vacation.

Debrena was going to visit her parents in Florida. She had asked me to go with her, but I told her that I wouldn't feel comfortable being away from my mother for that long. My mother had a stroke a few years ago, and except for some depression, she seemed to be all right. But my biggest fear was that she would become ill and I wouldn't be nearby to help her. Still, I knew I would miss Debrena and would count the days till she would return.

Did I want to dance anymore? "To be honest, I don't know. I got involved with the Young People's Dance Theater because my track coach said it might be a different kind of work out for me. I went down to Dominique's because you thought I should."

Debrena laughed softly. Her laughter was always music to my ears. "You make me sound like a bully."

"I didn't mean it like that, D. What I'm trying to say is dance was never my first love, especially being onstage. I had no problem with watching you do your thing. I've always enjoyed that."

"But you're so good, Lorrie. Right from the beginning, like I knew you would be."

"You always had more confidence in me than I had in myself."

"Don't be so hard on yourself. Aren't you glad you signed up for the Young People's Dance Theater?"

"If I hadn't done that, I would have never met you."

"Or Mr. Fred and all the great dance teachers like Miss Sally and everybody."

"But that was in school, D; when we were ten years old. I really didn't think about doing anything with it. When I ran into you with your mother in the mall, dance was not even a remote career possibility."

"You should never close your mind to self-expression, Lorrie. I'm not saying you have to be a dance diva like Dominique, but you should explore your talent."

"Like I said, I love dance, but not as much as you love it. You were awesome in Walter McCary's video, even though you didn't get to do any dancing."

Debrena laughed and held me tight around my waist. Her warm lips pressed into my neck, and before she spoke she kissed my bare shoulder. "I think that video made me more infamous than famous. After that music video every director wanted me to appear in their videos half naked. That's why I stopped even thinking about doing music videos; some people don't know the difference between a stripper and a dancer."

"They don't want to know," I said as I pushed my back into Debrena's front. Her full breasts were hot and heavy against my skin. "I'm just glad you didn't let them continue to use you like that."

"No more talk about me. Let's talk about you and what you should be doing."

"What do you mean? What should I be doing?"

"You have to follow your passion, Lorrie, like I'm following mine. Since so much has opened up for me I decided to go for it."

"Like your teaching?"

"That and so many other great things I never imagined."

After a moment of deep thought, I said, "I've always been interested in makeup. Even when I was a child. One time my mother spanked me because I used all of her Max Factor on my dolls. I wanted them to look beautiful."

"You're really good at face painting. Whenever we went out with the girls from Dominique's, everybody wanted you to do their makeup. You made us all look so beautiful."

"I really enjoyed doing that."

"Look, you should be doing more of that. The next video I do, if I ever do another one, I'm going to insist that they use you as my personal makeup artist. Although, when they see your dynamite figure, they will want you to dance."

We had been close friends since we were ten years old, and became lovers in the summer of 1999. With her close to me, holding me, she made me feel that I could do anything I set my mind to.

CHAPTER 5

Choice

I began my day at 6 A.M. I got out of bed and went across the room to my entertainment center. I put in my Graham Central Station CD and turned up the volume. The first cut was "Hair" that opened with a hard thumping bass guitar solo from Larry Graham, the leader of the group and a former member of the super group Sly and the Family Stone. This particular cut always got me going. As usual, I began my day with my "Dirty Dozens," a series of exercises that included sit-ups, push ups, squats, and some things I just made up as I went along.

All the music I used for these sessions were transferred from black vinyl records that had been part of my father's extensive record collection, a legacy he left to me in his will. My mother left no will, but there was nothing that I felt I needed from her. While she was alive she gave me everything I needed. Nobody saw it coming, although there should have been some investigation when my mother had to be rushed to the hospital with a dislocated shoulder a week before the tragedy that left me an orphan.

I threw myself into my calisthenics with an intensity that matched the hard driving 70's music that I listened to each and every day. I worked out for an hour, and with the sweat dripping like rain down my naked torso, I rushed to the shower because I wanted to spend some time in the darkroom before my meeting with Dany at NTA.

I mixed a smoothie in the blender in the small kitchen, and then pulled on a white tee shirt and some black sweat pants. I had to marvel at the way NTA set me up in the loft. I had all the space I needed and then some. They even built a darkroom, according to my precise specifications. In my special windowless area, I had a print side and a process side that enabled me to do any kind of work I wanted, from fine art to commercial photography. I never had to leave anything to chance or lab error because I had all the equipment to do everything.

In the darkroom, there was a pull string that bathed everything in a red light. On the print side was a timer high up on the wall, so I could read and check all of my exposure times. There was also a focus magnifier and a color analyzer. The floor was hardwood and easy to keep clean. I had print trimming, boxes of print paper, a roomy negative carrier, and a nice sized contact printing frame.

On the processing side, I had another timer, processing tongs, a thermometer, mixing rods, storage bottles, measuring beakers, processing tanks, all my chemicals, plastic funnels, a film dryer and processing unit, plus a sink with hot and cold running water.

I was like a screenwriter who could not only write the film he wanted, but he could produce it, direct it, edit it, score it, and manufacture it. I didn't know many artists like that. I knew I had it good at NTA.

That morning I developed prints for a shoot I did for *High Fashion* magazine, a spring preview of evening gowns from Paris, France. I hired a reed thin, Black model from the Bethann Hardison Modeling Agency. Although she was super model slim, she had round hips and full breasts. With a little persuasion, I got her to model topless in most of the shots, and this made a dramatic counterpoint to the silk tulle gowns she wore. I liked the way the round curve of her breasts met the slim line of her torso, especially when I photographed her from the back. When she wasn't topless, she wore an embroidered patent leather bustier with diamond details.

As the stylist for the shoot, Princess pulled together designs by Gaultier, Chanel, Versace, Givenchy, Valentino, and Christian Dior. Against the no-seam background was an artful arrangement of colorful silk flowers in standup brass flower holders. I could always count on Princess to do something stark and dramatic. For her, every shoot was a theatrical production. I shot five rolls of film. One of my favorite prints from that set was a back shot of the model in a black silk taffeta skirt with flower inserts. Her long back was bare and she wore long black gloves.

After I hung all the prints up to dry, I left the darkroom and slipped into some black leather running shoes.

I left my loft at 9:30 A.M. As I got into my black Lincoln truck, I didn't pull off until I put in my Jean Carn CD. Jean came on singing "Valentine Love" with Michael Henderson, and it calmed me right on down. I felt ready for Dany. I just hoped that she had a makeup artist. If not I could see some more wasted time in my future.

I had a great conversation with the people from *Urban Vibe* magazine and we had come up with some really good ideas. I had gotten a good feeling for what they wanted and was determined to give them more than they could ever imagine. The way I saw it, the client paid for my creativity. Any photographer could just point and shoot, but I saw myself as a "shooter," in the tradition of Gordon Parks, Bruce Weber, Herb Ritts, Jerry Avenaim, and Eddie "One Shot" Gibson, who I worked for in L.A. as a personal assistant before I went out on my own. These were great men who made every shot a work of art. They did fine art and commercial photography.

CHAPTER 6

As soon as I parked my ride in the front of the Nelson Talent Agency, Harrison Lyedecker came out of the building to greet me. It was almost like he was stalking me, waiting to ambush. He was at least six-five, the only man I knew that made me feel small. A Kean University student and an intern at NTA for the summer of 2000, he had been very helpful to me on the *High Fashion* shoot, serving as my personal assistant, loading my cameras, and helping me position my lights.

Before I could get out my Navigator, Lyedecker was at my driver's side. I rolled my window down to hear what he had to say.

"Choice, we got to talk," Lyedecker said, his words running together so fast I had to listen real hard.

"I'm here to meet with Dany, but if you want to talk after that—"

"It's got to be now, Choice. They're killing me in there. I'm making copies, delivering messages, taking minutes at meetings. Going out to get lunch orders. Everything but what I really want to do."

"And what is that?"

"I want to work with you, Choice."

"But you were hired to work for Dany and Carrie."

"That's before I knew how great it would be to work for you. You got me thinking about changing my major to fine arts."

I laughed. "Wait a minute; you can't change the whole direction of your life because you had a little fun on a shoot with me."

He looked behind to make sure that no one from the building was watching us and adjusted the fat knot in his necktie. "It's more than that, Choice. I got me a camera."

I laughed harder.

"Don't laugh, Choice. This is serious."

"I'm not laughing at you, Lyedecker. It's just that a lot of people say they want to do what I do, but are not willing to put in the time. This is not a hobby for me; it's a lifestyle. I eat, sleep, and drink this everyday. If a doctor told me that I had two days to live, I'd make sure that those two precious days were filled with shooting."

"I see where you're coming from. I'm not that deep into it, but I want to learn. I want to learn badly."

"I have something coming up, soon. Maybe I can get Dany to let you come in on that."

"Thanks, Choice."

"I can't promise you anything. I mean, like, you're an intern for NTA, not for me."

"You're with NTA."

"That's true, but you were hired to work for Dany and Carrie, let's understand that."

"I'm an intern, but I don't have any specific duties. They grab me for anything that no one else wants to do. All I got to do is be here from nine to five for my summer internship. Who knows where I'll be after this summer."

"I know where you'll be. You'll be back at Kean, working on that degree."

"I'll be working on a degree, but maybe not that degree."

"Whatever. Make sure you get a degree."

"You don't have a degree and you seem to be doing great."

"I'm doing all right. But don't get it twisted: this was what I was born to do, and I've been doing it since I got my first box camera at age nine. At this point I do what I do because I have no choice. This is all I know, this is all I want to know."

Lyedecker nodded like I had just delivered a sermon. I almost expected him to say, Amen, but he didn't. He just looked at me with worshipful eyes.

"Besides that, I'm sure your parents aren't paying all that good money at that university for you to become a shooter."

"My parents just want to see me gainfully employed."

"That's another reason for you to think twice about following in my footsteps. There are not many shooters who do this full-time. There's even fewer that make any real money. The only reason I'm halfway making it is because I do fine art and commercial photography. I'm versatile, and I hustle. I got this sweet thing with NTA, but I don't expect it to last forever."

"I'm sure your parents couldn't talk you out of following this dream."

He was about to say something else, but I cut him off by letting my window roll up.

CHAPTER 7

I found Dany in her office, dressed for business in a high neck white silk blouse, the jacket to her pinstriped pants suit draped over the back of her high back leather chair. She was on the phone with someone that was making her smile, and for her that usually meant some kind of business deal. She had a passion for big deals and big numbers. With her free hand, she motioned me to sit in the black leather chair in front of her desk. As I looked around the office, I noticed the slide projector on the coffee table in the middle of the room. The slides were in the carousel and the presentation was ready to go.

After hanging up the phone, Dany said, smiling broadly, "The numbers look real good." Then she had a concerned look on her face. "You okay?"

I fell into the chair in front of Dany's desk. "I'll be okay."

Dany looked at me like she didn't believe me.

I wasn't trying to be convincing. I had to deal with the fact that summer was the worse season of the year for me. My parents died in the summer of 1982; I had a big falling out with Eddie "One Shot" Gibson in the summer of 1995; I loved and lost Debrena in the summer of 1999.

"Well, maybe this will cheer you up," Dany began, "there are several makeup artists waiting to be interviewed."

I took a deep breath, and then smiled. What can I say? I'm an artist, and my emotions are very close to the surface. In a photo session that works well for me, but in the real world, I'm a magnet for hard times.

Dany stood up from her desk. "Listen to this, Choice," she began, smiling, picking up a sheet of paper. "I have you down here twice, for photography and film processing: five thousand for the pictures and fifteen hundred for the prints."

I smiled back at her, happy because she was happy. I hated to see her stressed because I was the one who usually stressed her out.

"Sounds good."

"That's not all," Dany went on. "I got twelve-fifty for Karen and another twelve-fifty for Princess."

I smiled. It was nice to know that my hair person and my stylist would be well taken care of. Too many times, Karen and Princess had to work for next to nothing. I couldn't wait to tell them that their hard work and patience with me was beginning to pay off. "Now all I need is a makeup artist," I had to add.

"Can you work that projector?"

I nodded.

"I'll get the lights," Dany said, walking from her desk.

This makeup artist's work was impressive. In a typical before and after slide show, she showed her versatility. What were once drab, ordinary faces became vibrantly alive. The makeup was not applied with a heavy hand. The women looked like real women, not lifeless mannequins. There was a sense of fun and I got the sense that I was appreciating the work of a master. I could see her fitting right in with Princess and Karen. There were some more slides, but I didn't need to see them. I shut down the projector.

"Had enough?" Dany called out to me in the darkness.

"Yeah."

When the lights came back on, Dany said, "I like her style. She's the only one who sent me this type of presentation, and she's local. You think she's worth twelve-fifty?"

"At least that," I said. "I love her work. She's hired. Now you need to call *Urban Vibe,* and let them know it's a go."

"Yes, sir," Dany said. "But she's only one out of a dozen. Don't you want to see the others?"

"No need. I'm more than satisfied. How do the numbers look on a two day prep?"

"I got it covered. I can get you fifteen hundred for two days of preparation." She smiled broadly, obviously satisfied.

I wanted to make sure that Karen and Princess got paid for all the running around they would have to do in the two days before the shoot. "Add another four-fifty to that, and I'll be very happy."

Dany looked down at the paper on her desk, and then up at me. "I think I can squeeze that out of the budget," she told me and I got the impression that she didn't have to squeeze too hard.

"The client is looking for a ten page spread," I said.

"I was at your sit down with the client."

"I'm going to need three models from Bethann."

Dany folded her arms under her breasts. She looked down at the paper on her desk one more time. "I can go four thousand per model."

That made me smile.

Then Dany added, "For a one day shoot, Choice."

"You know I work fast."

"Well, don't you at least want to meet this girl?" Dany asked as she sank back into her desk chair. "The makeup artist?"

That's when her phone rang. Dany spoke into the phone and became pleased from the news on the other end. "Okay, send her in."

CHAPTER 8

Because I was sitting with my back to the door, I had no idea who she stood up to greet. I stood and turned toward the door. I knew this was going to be my worst summer when Dany said, "This is your makeup artist, Lorrie Cunningham."

"Since when did you start doing makeup?"

"It has always been a hobby of mine," Lorrie said, looking straight at me.

"I...I...can't use you," I avoided eye contact with Dany who looked puzzled.

"I understand," Lorrie said.

"You're good, but it would never work out. I'm sorry you wasted your time." Then I turned toward Dany. "I'm sure we'll find someone before I leave for L.A."

Because I didn't know what else to say, I left.

Dany ran down the hall after me.

"What the hell is going on?" Dany asked as she caught up to me and grabbed my upper arm.

"Bad choice, Dany. Bad choice."

"She's great, Choice," Dany said, getting a little loud, which was not her style. "You said that yourself when you saw the slides. Now you act like this?"

I found it hard to look Dany in the eyes. "Let it go, Dany. I can't work with her. We'll have to find someone else. She's not the only makeup artist in the tri-state area. Besides, you said it yourself; she's one out of a dozen you have lined-up to be interviewed."

"Don't get smart with me. We don't have time for this foolishness. I don't want to lose this account, Choice!"

"We won't lose the account," I told her, getting a little loud myself. "I won't lose this client."

"It's a magazine, Choice. They have a deadline."

"We'll make the deadline, Dany!"

"Don't holler at me!"

"I'm not trying to holler at you, but you have to trust me on this one."

"Have you ever worked with Lorrie?"

I had almost worked with Lorrie on a calendar project I did for the Dominique St. Claire Dance Studio last summer. But things went crazy and I never got to work with her.

Dany stared at me. I knew we needed a makeup artist yesterday, and I knew that Lorrie Cunningham was the best person for the job. I also knew that having Lorrie around would be a constant reminder of Debrena. There was a strong possibility that I would run into Debrena, and as much as my heart ached for her, seeing her in the flesh was something I knew that I was not ready for.

"If I could use her I would," I told Dany, who stood before me looking hurt and confused.

"You have to tell me something. I've never seen you like this, Choice. This is not you."

I walked away.

"Choice!" Dany called out to me, but I kept walking.

CHAPTER 9

Lorrie

I entered the house with the key that Debrena had given me. She was in Florida, visiting her parents and had asked me to keep an eye on things. I brought in her mail and put it on the small table in the foyer. After getting shot down by Choice, all I wanted to do was be by myself to lick my wounds. I fell into a comfortable chair in the living room. I didn't want to go home right away because I knew that as soon as my mother saw my face she would know something was wrong. I didn't want to have a pity party, but I had to admit that Choice's rude dismissal had knocked the wind out of my sails.

I kicked my shoes off, and sat with my head thrown back. There was no surprise when the tears came. The only surprise was when my cell phone rang. I reached down into the Hermes bag that Debrena bought me and pulled out my cell phone.

"Hello?"

"Lorrie."

"Yes, Dany."

"First of all, I want to apologize for Choice Fowler's rude behavior."

"I caught him off guard; he never expected to see me at NTA."

"That's no excuse for rudeness, Lorrie. I don't want you to think that's the way we treat people at NTA."

"I know better, Dany. I just thank you for the time you spent with me."

"I'm just glad you had those slides."

I had to smile then. "My, um, girlfriend said I should do that. She says it's like a resume for a makeup artist."

"I never thought of it that way, but you know, she's right. Especially that before and after set. Very impressive."

"Well, maybe not impressive enough."

"Because of Choice's rudeness? Forget about Choice. When he saw the slides in my office, he was even more impressed than I was."

"Too bad he couldn't use me."

"That's what I'm calling to talk to you about. I called your house; your mother answered the phone. We had a nice little conversation. She gave me your cell number so that I could speak with you directly."

"She's not good at remembering messages."

"I see. I kept on calling her 'Mrs. Cunningham' and she insisted that I call her 'Miss Edna.'"

"She doesn't get out much, and she hardly gets any phone calls."

"Then I'll just have to call again."

"Did Choice tell you why he couldn't use me? I mean, why he didn't want to work with me?"

"I didn't ask. You're the best person for the job. Choice had to admit that. That's why he wants you."

I almost dropped my phone. "He wants me?"

"You're the best, Lorrie. We always go with the best at NTA."

"But Choice…," I began, my face hot, "I didn't think he'd ever mention my name again."

"He called back two hours after you left and said, 'Let's go with Lorrie.'"

"Dany, I can't believe this."

"I said, 'Choice, it will serve you right if Lorrie turns you down, the way you showed your black ass.' Choice had to go with you, Lorrie."

My body tingled.

"So, I have to ask: Would you consider working with Choice? He has a hair person and a stylist, but he really needs you. But if you say no, I'll understand."

"Yes!"

"You mean, yes you'll work with the ignorant Choice Fowler?"

"Yes, Dany. Yes. Yes. Yes."

"You only had to say it once, girl."

We laughed, and I felt that I had made a new friend.

CHAPTER 10

Choice

Now that's my kind of music," Curtis said as we sat in Malika's Place, enjoying an after work set in the upscale soul food restaurant. The recorded music was low, a perfect complement to the lively crowd that frequented the place on this summer Friday night. "You know who that is?"

"No."

"Choice, that is Herbie Hancock. The greatest piano player that ever lived."

"When did he die?"

Curtis laughed, "Brother Man, Herbie Hancock is very much alive. I mean he's been around a long time, with Miles Davis, John Coltrane, jazz giants like that, but he's still on the scene. What you're listening to now is 'Masqualero,' a jazz classic."

I thought the tune sounded like classical music, but didn't share that with Mr. Know-It-All-Curtis.

"Yes, that's my man. I invited you to dinner because I wanted to holler at you before you made your way off to La La Land."

"Why can't you just call it L.A.?"

"La La Land sounds better, especially as it pertains to you. You get out there and you forget to represent."

He was talking about Londa Newberry again. I had made the mistake of showing Curtis some nude photos I had shot of Londa. They were just test shots, but she was there in her butt naked splendor, and Curtis just couldn't get her out of his mind. "How do you want me to represent, Curtis?"

"Brother Man, you know you should be hitting that. Man, you should be knocking the bottom out of that L.A. honey. Now I never met her, but those pictures you reluctantly showed me—I'll be damned if she don't look like Vanessa Williams."

I had to agree with Curtis. At five-six and a size four or small six, Londa, an aspiring actress and trade show model, had it going on. I couldn't wait to get back to L.A. to spend some time with her. We had been friends for years, nothing sexual, just friends. But Curtis couldn't understand that.

Curtis made a fist and aimed it at me. "Make me proud, Choice. Represent for the brothers on the East Coast. Let her know the Black man is a king on the land and in the bedroom."

Sometimes he gave me the impression that he would jump between the thighs of any woman that opened up for him. I was always into quality more than quantity. But I knew Curtis would never understand that. He had even suggested that I sleep with Princess and Karen because, "They both dig you like babies dig mother's milk."

"Let me get to L.A. I'll show you what to do," Curtis continued. He sat across from me dressed in a gray cotton two button suit, gray cotton shirt, yellow-and-white silk tie, and sported a Hamilton watch he told me one of his "honeys" had bought for him.

Because Curtis wouldn't have it any other way, I had to dress up to hang out with him. I wore a double breasted white linen jacket over a dark blue tee shirt and black dress pants, and on my feet were expensive Martin Dingman shoes that he had talked me into buying. I couldn't wait for Londa to see me like this; she also felt I should do more with my wardrobe, but she wasn't as obnoxious as Curtis. I never thought that clothes made the man, but I had to admit, I felt pretty good sitting up there in Malika's Place.

"That reminds me," I said, digging into my front pants pocket. I pulled out a set of keys and pulled off one key. "Here's a copy of my house key. I'ma need you to look after my place until I get back. Just stop by every so often to make sure everything's cool."

"Am I my brother's keeper?" Curtis asked as he placed the key into his front pants pocket.

Before I could respond Curtis cut me off. "Now listen to this," Curtis said, bringing me back to the music. "I know this is funky enough for you."

I listened to the music before I asked, "What's the name of that tune? It does sound familiar."

"Everybody has recorded it," Curtis said. "It's 'Watermelon Man'; you probably heard Mongo Santamaria's version of it. But it was also recorded by the big bands of Woody Herman, Si Zenter, and Maynard Ferguson."

I didn't know any of those names, but Curtis Walker was impressed enough for both of us.

"Yeah, you hang with me and you'll be all right."

"Yeah, yeah. Besides that you owe me a meal."

"Brother Man, you're never going to let me forget that."

"It was your dinner party, Curtis."

Curtis looked like a man in great pain. "You know sometimes when you're trying to impress a honey, you go that extra mile."

"Is that so? All I know is that I was invited to your condo for dinner and came out of your place stravin' like Marvin."

Curtis shook his head in amazement. "You just won't let that go."

"I was really looking forward to that dinner party. You know how we Black people do. I didn't eat anything all that day, just drank some water, so I could get my grub on." I almost laughed out loud when I saw the pained expression on Curtis's face. "And the honeys, as you call them, were all looking real tight."

Curtis leaned forward and folded his hands in front of his face.

"But the food, Curtis."

"I told you, my lady of the moment picked the menu."

"The food, Curtis. What was she thinking, man?"

"You know, sometimes Black people need to try something new."

"She was just as proud, escorting me to the buffet table. If she smiled any harder, she would've pulled a muscle in her cheeks.

'You must try the Tako Sunomono,' your honey told me. Tako Sunomono, Curtis. That was sliced octopus, with cucumber, and vinegar sauce. Yum, yum, good."

I saw a smile creeping around the corners of his mouth.

"But she wouldn't stop there. Oh, no, she heard I was your best friend from the job so she had to impress me." Then I spoke in a loud falsetto, 'Or perhaps you'd like to try the Futo Maki? That's egg, crab cakes, carrot, kampyo, and fish powder' and all I'm thinking is: where's the fried chicken and potato salad, with the biscuits, and the sweet potato pie?"

Curtis's lips began to tremble, and then he laughed out loud. "Nigga, you ain't shit!"

I laughed along with him.

"You can take a nigga out of the country…"

"Yeah. Yeah. I know the rest."

"That's why I brought you here."

"To give a brother a real meal?"

"Yeah. Also to congratulate you. Dany told me that you pulled your team together. Got a hot makeup artist. I heard she's fine too."

"And you say that to say what?"

"I want to meet her, Brother Man."

I had second thoughts about hiring Lorrie. In the back of my mind I thought there might be some way for me to use Lorrie to get back with Debrena.

"What you say, Choice? Can I get the digits?"

I ignored him and enjoyed the music.

CHAPTER 11

O nce I got to Los Angeles, I hailed a cab at the airport, carrying a garment bag and a smaller bag, more than enough for a L.A. weekend. I told the cabdriver to take me to the Convention Center where I was to meet Londa. She was working a trade show, a Boat Expo, featuring luxury yachts and mini-seminars on better boating. When I got there admission was free because Londa had put my name on the V.I.P. list. Once inside I had to marvel at the enormity of the Convention Center and the fact that there were at least twenty yachts in there, not to mention the trade show booths that featured marine products that any hardcore boater just had to have.

Because I was allowed to leave my luggage near the front of the establishment, I was able to walk around the floor unburdened. It wasn't hard to find Londa. Even among all the other beauties, she stood out. They all wore patriotic designer swimwear, two pieces, and one pieces that covered everything, but still created a certain sexual tension that I, for one, found hard to ignore. Londa stood near what a banner proclaimed as a Sea Ray Week-ender yacht, a sleek white on the outside and an earth tone brown on the inside. Of course, she had a little group of

White men around her, but I couldn't believe that they really thought she knew anything about boats. She tossed her sandy colored hair and laughed, entertaining them. She was good at her job, which paid four hundred and fifty dollars per day.

I watched her work, and my body felt warm like I was about to meet someone new. I had never seen her dressed quite like that. She wore the American flag as a two piece string bikini.

I got the eerie feeling that I wasn't alone. I looked over to my right and found a White man whose eyes were so dead on her that I felt like I had to shield her from him with my body. He was one of the few men in the center with a suit on. His only nod to the casualness of all the other White men there was the fact that he wore no necktie. His steady gaze only lifted off Londa when he caught me staring at him. Playing it real cool, he nodded at me.

If I were her man, a long stare like that from a stranger would be cause for a beat down and I sensed he knew that because he blushed red from his round chin and semi-bald head. I looked over at Londa, then back at him, but by that time he had disappeared into the crowd.

"You look nice," Londa said when she finally got over to me.

"Thank you," I said, knowing she would like me in my white linen jacket that I wore over a dark brown tee shirt that matched my dark brown summer suede shoes. I also wore white linen pants. I wasn't a fashion plate like Curtis Walker, but with my long dreadlocked hair, I knew I stood out. "Aren't you breaking some law," I jokingly asked, "wearing the American flag like that?"

Londa laughed, her green eyes sparkling and her lips painted a beautiful pink. Her skin was smooth and honey colored. "No one has said anything. Yet."

I looked around the vast auditorium. "How many men you think are really in the market to buy a boat?"

Londa looked around. "I couldn't begin to guess."

Before I could ask my follow up question we had company.

"Choice, this is Leon Parker," Londa said.

Leon was the White man that was staring at Londa like she was a free meal.

"Leon heads Parker Productions, and provides models for trade shows, promotions, photography, and the fashion industry," Londa continued.

I wasn't impressed.

"I've been in business for ten years now," Leon told me, standing close to Londa. "I operate in many markets, including Oregon, Washington, Nevada, Texas, and Arizona."

"You do get around," I commented.

He babbled on letting me know that he provided models for various special events, including wine and liquor tasting, golf tournaments, beauty pageants, and sporting events like the Super Bowl and the World Series. I feigned boredom, and Leon finally left us alone.

"This is a skimpy costume," Londa had to admit, "but it isn't the worse thing I had to wear for a promotion."

The worse was when she had to dress up as a drumstick for a promotion in Chicago. "We had to wear white panty hose and a drum stick costume."

I smiled and shook my head. "The things we artist have to do to make a living."

"By the way, how was your flight?"

"My flight was all right. I got here safe and sound, and I can't wait to spend some time with you. How soon can we get out of here?"

Before she could answer, Leon was back. "If you don't let my favorite hostess go, I'm going to have to put you in a stars and stripes bikini," Parker said, making a weak joke, but I got his message.

"I'll be out on the terrace," I told Londa. "Let me know when you're ready to roll."

Then I walked away, not looking back at Londa, or Leon.

CHAPTER 12

I looked for a door that would let me out onto the terrace surrounding the L. A. Convention Center. I had to find a door that would not set off a fire alarm. Outside I saw a small group of men and women who had stepped out to smoke cigarettes. I joined them on the slate gray terrace, but stayed away so that their noxious smoke didn't drift over to me.

At age twenty-eight I felt that I was not where I was supposed to be, especially when compared to someone like Londa. She owned her own home, and I'm sure she had a fat bank account. As for me, the work was coming in, but that was due more to NTA than any efforts on my own part. Maybe it was jet lag, but melancholy suddenly made me stressed out and irritable. I stood with my hands on the low wall that surrounded the terrace and looked out into the slightly foggy sky. It was a hot, airless afternoon and I felt that if I didn't breathe deeply I wouldn't get enough fresh air.

Suddenly, laughter came from somewhere behind me and I knew it wasn't from the smokers I had crashed in on. This new force was at once strange and familiar.

After the laughter, a voice called out to me, "Choice?"

I didn't have to turn around to know it was Janis Wilson. When I did turn I found her excusing herself from a small laughing group, so that she could come over to me. She wore a neutral gray dress with a boat neck collar that hugged her like a lover. The last time I had seen her was the previous summer in Elizabeth, New Jersey. "What are you doing here?" I asked.

From an expensive, fancy handbag, Janis pulled out a card. "I'm promoting a little jazz set here tonight. A jazz trio from the Bay Area." Janis held the card out in front of me, but because I didn't want to take it, she shrugged and put it back into her handbag. "Are you just visiting or home to stay?"

"Visiting a friend," I said, angry because she was acting like she never did me any harm.

Janis looked at me. "You're not still holding a grudge against me because of that tape?" She frowned. "The way I see it, I did you a favor, Choice. You needed to know who Debrena Allen really is."

A picture of Debrena spread out half naked on a bed with a woman's head between her thighs flashed in my mind. This was actually recorded on a videotape that was left in my mailbox.

Janis looked behind herself, then back to me. "That girl is a freak, Choice. You really needed to know that. It wasn't like you were in love with her."

I stared at Janis. Hard.

"Don't tell me you loved her, Choice," Janis shook her head in disbelief. "I can't believe it. You just met her that summer. I—"

"Leave me alone! Just get the hell out of my face!"

"Debrena can't love you. Debrena loves women too much to love any man. Believe me, I know her type."

"Shut your damn mouth!" I shouted. "I don't need your advice."

Janis smirked.

"You are the last person on this earth I want to discuss Debrena with."

Janis laughed and I felt like breaking her face with my fists.

"You know, Choice," Janis went on, her voice soft and seductive. "You can't change a 'ho into a house wife, and you can say the same thing about a freak. Once a freak, always a freak."

I turned away from Janis. I was so angry my hands shook. "*I don't need your help,"* I told her over my shoulder, enunciating every word.

Janis laughed. Again.

I turned around and moved toward Janis. Just then, Londa stepped out onto the terrace. Her presence calmed me down, reminded me that I had never done bodily harm to any woman.

Janis walked pass Londa, who now wore a white robe over her stars and stripes bikini.

CHAPTER 13

W hat was that all about?" Londa asked.

"I just wasn't ready to see her."

"An old girlfriend?"

I laughed out loud. "Never that. Her name is Janis Wilson. She works with a big record company here in L.A. She handles some acts on the side, as a manager. I guess you can say that I'm not a fan of her business practices."

Londa nodded, noticing the way I held my body. "I can't leave now. I want to, but I can't."

"I'll be all right."

"I'll be out of here soon."

I nodded.

"But if you want, you can wait for me at my place."

I tried to smile, "I can wait for you."

"No, Choice. I don't want you to do that. You look too stressed."

Londa dug her hands into the pocket of her long white robe. She handed me the keys to her vehicle. "The keys to my house are also on that ring."

I was so humbled that I didn't know what to say.

"Get out of here, you know my car," Londa instructed me.

"I'm parked in front of the building in the front row of the visitors' parking lot. I'll meet you at my house."

"How will you get home?"

"One of the girls will drop me off."

I hugged her tightly, and then reluctantly left her.

I got my luggage from the front of the auditorium and then made my way out of the building. I found her SUV where she said I would. I threw my things into the long back seat and steered up one snaking road after another on the way to her house. Occasionally, the Hollywood sign would peek out from between the hills. I felt that I was home when I pulled up to the curb in front of Londa's wide ranch style home.

I didn't notice any major changes in the living room. I went over to the clean pine wood entertainment center and looked at Londa's collection of music. She was a big Metallica fan so there was *Reload, Load, Kill 'Em All,* and *Black Album.* On the wall to my left was a poster announcing a Metallica performance at Phoenix Theatre in Petaluma, California. One of her greatest fan moments was in 1996 when she saw Metallica live at Slim's, a small club in San Francisco. The performance was beamed across the globe live by a web cast crew. Her collection included Megadeth, Guns 'N Roses, Jane's Addiction, Red Hot Chilli Peppers, System Of A Down, Van Halen, and Dead Kennedys.

I shook my head in amazement because after all the years I had known her, I still couldn't understand her taste in music. I dug into one of my bags and found the antidote to the White heavy metal disease that had affected Londa's Black mind. Perhaps I should say half Black mind because her mother was White and her father was Black.

I always traveled with my music. Before I continued I injected some sweet soul music into the entertainment system. When Peabo Bryson came oozing out of the speakers, singing "I'm So Into You" I knew I would be all right. But before I left the living room I looked at the wall and saw that Londa had framed a picture I took of her some years ago.

It was a montage of three shoots: One head shot, one shot of her sitting in a chair, casually dressed in jeans, bare foot, and a

Terry B.

long white shirt over a white tee, and one shot of her just smiling her sweet smile, dressed in a long white button-up shirt, with a plaid collar. On the picture was a legend that read: LONDA NEWBERRY. HEIGHT 5' 6". BUST: 34. WAIST: 23. HIPS: 34. DRESS SIZE: 4 OR A SMALL 6. SHOE: 6. HAIR: SANDY. EYES: GREEN. I wondered where she kept the nudes I had done. I remembered that it was her idea, and she wasn't self-conscious as she modeled for me. The camera loved the fullness of her body and her smooth curves.

In the bedroom that I used as a guestroom, I noticed that all my prints were still on the wall; not photos that I took, but photos by photographers I admired like Sally Mann, David LaChapelle, Herb Ritts, and Howard Schatz. There was even a framed print by Eddie "One Shot" Gibson; *I have to talk Londa into getting rid of that one,* I thought. I had to admit, no matter what I thought about One Shot as an individual, he was a damn good shooter. On a table near the bed was a stack of magazines I had left behind that included *American Photo*, *Outdoor Photography*, *Studio Photography Design*, *PC Photo and Aperture*.

Back in the living room on my way to the long gallery-like kitchen, I was greeted by the sexy soul sounds of the Delfonics singing, "I Don't Want To Make You Wait." I had to stop in my tracks to listen to that one, then right after that, Major Harris, who later in his career sang with the Delfonics, came on singing, "Love Won't Let Me Wait." I had to pull myself away when Teddy Pendergrass came on singing, "Come Go With Me."

I wanted to make a little culinary magic in the kitchen. I put together a stir fry with zucchini, mushrooms, onions, celery, peppers, and carrots.

I planned to grill some chicken breasts I found in the frig, but then I decided to go veggie. I found some sweet treats that made me weak in the knees with pleasure. Londa and I liked to eat healthy, but we also had a weakness for desserts.

Heart be still, I said to myself as I looked upon the sinfully delicious treats that would take us through the weekend: cherry almond cheese cake tarts, chiffon cake, carrot cake, and my personal favorite, Dutch chocolate cake.

Like Superman being exposed to Kryptonite, I weakly pulled myself out of the kitchen and into the living room. The only thing that saved me was the soothing, life affirming music that came out of the speakers. Lying on Londa's black leather couch, I let the music wash over me: "Hello" by Lionel Ritchie; "Through The Fire" by Chaka Khan; "You Are My Lady" by Freddie Jackson; "One In A Million" by Larry Graham; "Angel" by Angela Winbush; "Don't Say No Tonight" by Eugene Wilde.

I was in a soul music session coma by the time Londa finally got home. She looked like a perfect angel as she stood in the doorway. She was dressed casual bohemian in a pink tank top beneath a short denim jacket, over a ruffled white cotton skirt, and on her feet were pink and white sling backs. "Now that is the perfect picture of a man in R&B paradise," Londa said, smiling broadly. "I was a little worried about you, but I see that you have gotten yourself together."

I couldn't move from the couch, I was too relaxed. "Dinner is ready when you are."

Londa laughed out loud. "You are too cute. I'll set the table, and light some candles."

That sounded all right to me.

CHAPTER 14

Whenever I came to visit Londa, she let me take the lead in our meals and entertainment. I did all the cooking, and she let me play all the 60's, 70's, and 80's music I brought with me. As for film entertainment, I had that covered too.

"I'm almost afraid to ask what you brought with you," Londa said as she sat across from me at the dinner table. She always teased me about the violent nature of the films I enjoyed.

"I got *Shaft,* starring Samuel L. Jackson, directed by John Singleton," I smiled from ear to ear.

"You and your bootlegs," Londa said and smiled as she shook her head. She was totally relaxed, her jean jacket in a nearby chair and her shoes across the room in a corner.

"I get to see all the new movies and never have to leave my house," I explained to her as I chewed on my last bite of carrot cake. "I even got a copy of *The Nutty Professor,* starring Eddie Murphy."

"Choice, you really know how to treat a lady," Londa said, teasing me like only she could. "Did you bring me a picture? You always bring me a picture for my bedroom."

"Thanks for reminding me," I said as I rose from the table.

"You don't have to get it now," Londa said, motioning for me to sit back down.

"Let me get it out of my luggage," I said as I started to walk out of the kitchen. I returned with a soft framed black and white photo by Howard Schatz. I held it up high so Londa could get the total effect. "You can change the frame if you want to; it was easier for me to carry it this way."

"Nice, very expressive," was Londa's comment and I knew she was genuine. "But why does she have to be naked?"

"This is a classic Howard Schatz shot, from his book *Passion and Line.*" It was a nude of ballerina Shannon Chain, a White woman on her toes with one leg back, her back arched with her head and arms thrown back. There were a lot of dark shadows and her body looked like a white marble sculpture. Schatz shot the photo with a Hasselband camera with a 120mm lens, and printed it out on multigrade paper. "And she's not naked, she's nude."

"She seems very free, I'll keep it, but you must send me some of your work."

"I will, when I have something that I think you need to see."

"Speaking of dancers," Londa began. "What's happening with your dancer friend, what's her name? Debrena, right?"

I sat down heavily at the table. "The less said about her, the better."

"I know you told me that the two of you broke up, but sometimes, with a little distance, things work out."

"I haven't seen her in over a year, Londa. I think that's enough distance, and more than enough time."

"In the beginning, you sounded so hopeful, like she was the one."

"I was wrong."

"You never did tell me what happened."

"There's nothing to tell. We had a good run, and now it's over. Finished. End of story."

"Then why are you so angry?"

I laughed, amused because my friend knew me too well.

"Maybe this is not good after dinner conversation," Londa suggested.

"I can't duck and dodge your questions, especially when we've always been so straight with each other."

"Choice, you're the only one that would let me call long distance and cry over the lovers I've lost. I always said that I would like to return the favor, give you a shoulder to cry on."

"I never thought I'd need that."

"Maybe you don't even need it now, but if you do, I'm here."

"That's good to know."

"I hate to see you stressed, Choice. The last time you were so stressed was when you couldn't find a makeup artist for this job you wanted to do."

"I have a makeup artist now. I signed her before I left for L.A."

"So that problem is solved."

"But another problem has presented itself." That was when I told her about my dilemma of using Debrena's close friend, Lorrie, as part of my team. Of course, I didn't tell Londa how close they were.

After I finished, Londa said, "I don't think you should deny Lorrie this opportunity if she's good."

I had to nod my head in agreement.

"She is good, right?"

"One of the best I've ever seen."

"So when you get back home you'll be able to jump right into that project. I know when I'm stressed work is the best thing for me."

"Yeah, but I know you'd rather be in front of the camera, making movies, rather than walking around in skimpy costumes, playing hostess."

Londa looked at me with a hurt expression on her face. "You make what I do sound so shallow."

That was the great thing about our relationship, we could tell each other whatever we had on our minds and not worry about permanently hurt feelings. "All I'm saying is that you're better than that. I've seen you onstage, but I know you want movies."

"I need movies. My soul aches for it."

We talked about her hopes for a film career, but for some reason, Londa brought us back to Debrena. "We don't have to talk about her if it makes you uncomfortable."

"I don't see how talking about it can help. Debrena has moved on."

"Have you moved on?" Londa asked studying my face.

"I have no choice."

"You're not answering my question."

"Now, this is when I'm supposed to call you a 'nosey bitch' and tell you to mind your own business."

Londa smiled. "I don't allow anybody, not even a good friend like you, to curse me out in my own house. But if you don't want to talk about it, it's okay. Besides, it's late. I should take a shower, but I'm too tired. And I'm used to my own funk."

I laughed because I could always count on Londa to keep it real.

"I'll talk to you in the morning, Choice. But not too early. Right now I think you need some quiet time. I'm going to hang my new picture in my bedroom. Good night."

"Good night," I whispered as Londa walked away.

CHAPTER 15

After a night of tossing and turning, I decided to get up. Knowing I would not return to bed, I dug into my luggage for some exercise clothes. I grabbed a washed out gray muscle shirt and a pair of even more washed out cutoffs. I then walked through Londa's house, and although it was after ten in the morning, her bedroom door was closed.

I pushed open the glass doors that lead out to her wide sundeck. The most notable thing, besides the large umbrella and the round glass table and the lounge chairs beneath it, was the large wooden box that housed her hot tub. It was an Emerald 599 that sat seven people comfortably and had twenty-three jets to make the water nice and bubbly. I enjoyed the hot tub, but that morning I looked forward to having the freedom of the deck to work out. I did my Dirty Dozen and I didn't notice Londa until I had finished my work out.

"How long have you been standing in the doorway?" I asked as she threw me a big, fluffy, white towel.

"Long enough to make me feel guilty about the way I made a pig of myself last night," Londa told me, and then patted her flat stomach.

"I thought you ate like that just to make me happy," I said teasingly, "to assure me that my culinary skills were up to par."

"As my country cousins would say, 'You put your foot in that meal.' Everything was excellent."

"You're just saying that because it's true," I said jokingly, and then I really noticed Londa, especially the way her long bare, honey colored legs peeked out of her long white robe. I wondered if she were naked under that robe.

"I love a man with confidence," Londa said and then laughed. The laughter was music to my ears and the words "love a man" stuck with me longer than they needed to. "Choice, I was wondering: I'd like to take a ride and go down to Santa Monica."

If Londa was thinking about Santa Monica, she had to be thinking about lunch at Michael's, the restaurant we visited at least once during my visits. The thought of dining at Michael's thrilled me, but I didn't want to go down there and have to rush back. "Aren't you needed at the boat expo?" I had to ask. "I don't want to be the cause of you losing money."

"I can handle Leon," she assured me. "I told him I had a house guest, that I needed this weekend off."

"Did he know I was your house guest?"

"He knows now," Londa said, her green eyes sparkling with mischief. "He thought you were my man, my boyfriend. He said I shouldn't wear myself out. I had to let him know we were like brother and sister."

"You let him ask about your sex life?"

"Choice, I don't have a sex life," Londa sighed. "Or at least not with a man."

I looked away. I wasn't exactly burning up the sheets myself. After Debrena there was no one I wanted to be intimately involved with. "I just find it hard to believe that a beautiful woman like you would have trouble finding male companionship."

"I can always find male companionship, Choice. It takes a lot more than a male's presence to satisfy me sexually. I have to be comfortable, and that takes time. I have had many offers, but I'm not one to jump into bed with any Tom, Dick, or Harry."

I laughed.

Londa raised a curious eyebrow at me. "You laughing at me, Choice Fowler?"

"No, nothing like that," I assured her. "I'm just amused, surprised really. I've never heard you talk about your sex life."

"You've never asked me about my sex life."

"That's true," I had to admit, feeling a little uncomfortable because I didn't know where Londa was going with this sex talk. I used the towel she gave me to rub my suddenly hot face.

"You up for it?"

I hesitated.

"I'm talking about Michael's," Londa told me, smiling. "You *up* for lunch at the restaurant?"

I nodded my head slowly.

"I'm going to take a shower and put on some clothes," Londa announced, and then she turned to go back into the house.

I wondered again if she was naked under that long white robe.

CHAPTER 16

It was Londa's idea to get dressed up because as she explained it, "I seldom get a chance to do it." Because I wasn't a dress up kind of guy this meant wearing the outfit I had worn to dinner with Curtis before I left New Jersey for Los Angeles. In the guestroom I dressed and pulled my hair back and tied it with a long, black, leather, thick string. I came into Londa's living room wearing my double breasted, white linen jacket over a blue muscle shirt, with black dress pants, and my Martin Dingman shoes.

Londa didn't keep me waiting. When she came into the living room, all I could say was, "Simply beautiful."

She wore an oriental style, floral print silk mini-dress that left most of her arms bare, along with her long, smooth shapely legs. On her feet were black slides; in her hand was a white fabric bag with floral embroidery and a bamboo handle. *China doll*, I thought as I looked at her standing before me.

"I like to get dressed up sometimes," Londa said as she grabbed the hand I extended to her. She held onto my hand as we walked out to her SUV. She handed me her keys and I opened the door for her. "You drive," she suggested.

We listened to a Marvin Gaye CD I had brought with me as we made our way down to Santa Monica. When we got to

Michael's, we went directly to our favorite spot, a secluded patio that was surrounded by rock walls and green plants with thick glossy leaves and trees. I ordered pan roasted chicken with all the tasty extras and Londa ordered the grilled salmon with wilted chard and horse radish potatoes.

"Thank you," Londa said as she sat across from me, putting her hand bag on the white wicker table.

"For what?"

"For being so patient with me. I don't have a man in my life right now because of that. Most men want to rush things. Go right to the bedroom, I don't want that. I won't have that."

"But you're not opposed to the bed action?" I asked, more curious than I felt I had the right to be.

"Not opposed at all," Londa said with a mischievous glint in her eyes. "As a matter of fact, I welcome that. When the time is right."

"Who determines when the time is right?"

"We'll both know," Londa said and then lowered her eyes like she had exposed too much of herself. "I don't know about you, but I need a drink."

After signaling for a waiter, Londa ordered a Bellini cocktail, which contained white peach puree and Italian sparkling wine, according to our menu. "Have a drink with me," she suggested. I ordered a Virgin Frozen Bikini, getting the peach tree schnapps, the peach nectar, orange and lemon juice, and skipping the vodka and champagne, I had to stay sober to get us back to her place safely.

"Choice, are you seeing anyone now?" Londa asked as we waited for our drinks.

"No one. And you?"

"No one wants me."

"You're a beautiful woman. Maybe the time is not right now."

"When will it be right, Choice? I'm so hungry for love. I feel like I'm drying up inside."

Before I could comment, the waiter returned with our drinks.

After the waiter left, Londa proposed a toast: "To better days and more love."

I gently tapped her glass with mine, and then we both drank.

"What do you think my problem is?" Londa asked. "You tell me that I'm a beautiful woman, but I haven't had a man in a very long time."

"Because they move too fast, you told me that."

"It's more than that. I mean, some women set rules for themselves. Like no sex until the third date or something like that."

"But you don't do it like that."

"I want to be spontaneous. Maybe that's the problem. Maybe I'm being too idealistic. I don't think too many men can deal with an old fashioned girl like me. I can't help it, Choice. I want to be respected the morning after."

"Are you thinking about getting married and settling down?"

"No. No, it's not about that; I still want my career. I still believe I can be a big screen actress. Am I being realistic?"

"I think you are."

"Maybe I don't have sex appeal."

"Sex appeal, Londa? On a scale of one to ten, I rate you a thirteen."

Londa laughed out loud, obviously touched.

"I find that hard to believe coming from you, of all people."

"What do you mean?"

"Choice, you've proven time and time again that you have the power to resist me."

"I don't understand."

"You photographed me naked and you didn't even make a pass. You would've if you found me sexy."

I chuckled. "I try not to mix business with pleasure. I especially don't like to mix friendship with pleasure. Besides, those were just test shots."

"So I won't have to worry about seeing any of those naked pictures of me in *Hustler* magazine, in the Beaver Hunt section?"

"Not unless I want you to sue me. I can't use anything unless you sign a release. Besides, I gave you the negatives. I didn't think you wanted any nude shots in your portfolio, especially not the portfolio you'd take to movie studios to get film work."

"I have to stop being such a prude. All the new actresses do nude scenes today. I got a lot of damn nerve thinking I would be exempt from that."

"You're a good actress," I told her forcefully, recalling the many times I had seen her at Los Angeles playhouses. "You don't have to sell sex, especially when you can sell your talent."

Londa smiled sadly. "Thanks. You should be with someone. You'd make a woman very happy." Then she finished her drink. "I think I'll have another one of these."

CHAPTER 17

On the drive back to Londa's house she was strangely quiet. As soon as we arrived she went into her bedroom and closed the door behind her. I felt a little sorry for Londa because her loneliness was obvious, and there was nothing I thought I could do to help her, without overstepping the bounds of our friendship.

In the guestroom I took off my dress clothes and hung them up. Then I put on a tee shirt and some shorts. I decided to step out on her sundeck. I spent a little time out there, checking out the landscape that surrounded her house. I was about to head back into the house when Londa came out onto the sundeck. She wore a black vee neck tee shirt that fit her like a mini-dress.

As I looked at her, it was easy for me to see her in the company of young, hot actresses out that summer, like Jasmine Guy, Halle Berry, Nia Long, Maia Campbell, and Viveca A. Fox. She had the looks and the talent to compete with any of them. In her hands were two glasses filled with what looked like orange juice. "I brought you something," she told me as she handed me a glass.

The drink burned my throat; it was orange juice mixed with vodka. "Whoa!"

"Surprise," she said, then sipped her drink.

As Londa looked over the rim of her glass, I got the impression that we were about to move out of the "friend zone." When we emptied our glasses she took them, setting them on a nearby table. "We'll have some more later."

Londa turned away from me and walked to the hot tub. I couldn't help but notice the back of her thick, shapely legs. Londa grabbed the neck of her tee with both hands and pulled it over her head, and then completely nude, she stepped into the hot tub. In seconds, she had the jets full blast and the water up to her neck. "Join me, please."

I pulled my tee shirt off, and then stripped out of my shorts. I was nude and semi-erect when I climbed into the hot tub. "You sure you want to do this?" I asked as the water swirled around us.

"Shut up and kiss me," Londa insisted as she moved toward me.

We kissed before as friends, but this was different. I held onto her small shoulders and bent my head to taste her mouth. There was the taste of orange juice and vodka, and a sort of sweetness that made me eagerly probe her mouth with my tongue. Her body in the water was hot and sleekly wet. Her breasts were heavy against me and her thick, erect nipples stabbed me softly. I refused to let go of her mouth as my hands moved up and down her body. Her moans were soft in my ear as I felt the warm wetness between her wide spread thighs.

"I want—" Londa began, but stopped abruptly when I stuck two fingers inside her. With her thighs wide, she rode my fingers. To keep her close to me, I palmed her hot, bare ass. She climaxed suddenly and shuddered violently, catching me completely by surprise.

"Oh, no," Londa gasped as she pushed me away. It was as if her sexual hunger had gotten the best of her and she was fighting for control. She fell into me and I lifted her head so that I could claim her mouth again.

Are you thinking with the right head? I asked myself as her hot belly pressed against my hard-on. Londa sensed my hesitation and read it as rejection.

"You don't want me, nobody wants me," Londa sobbed as she pushed me away.

"Londa, wait." She scrambled out of the tub and grabbed her tee shirt. Not even bothering to put it on, she ran into the house.

I cursed myself for being a fool as I climbed out of the tub. We had moved out of the friend zone and I knew there was no turning back. I walked nude into the house and found her in her bedroom. She was looking out of the window. Her full back was exposed to me. She held her tee shirt to the front of her body.

"You don't have to have sex with me," Londa said, her voice filled with pain and embarrassment.

I held onto her small shoulders as I talked to her back. "I want to," I told her. And to let her know I meant business I pressed my hard-on into her back. She brushed up against me when I took a hand off her shoulder and put it on her hot, flat belly. She was so hot it felt like she was sick with fever. I spun her around and the tee shirt fell to the floor between us. There were tears in her eyes and her small, well shaped body trembled beneath my fingers. I kissed her again as I let my fingers fall down between her thighs.

"I'm so wet," Londa told me. "I don't need any foreplay."

I nodded and walked her back to her bed. As she lay there with her legs spread wide, I grabbed myself and said, "I don't have any protection."

"In the bottom drawer," Londa told me, and then looked away from me like she was embarrassed.

There was a box of twelve. When I took one out, eleven remained. I slid on a condom. Then I entered her and she wrapped her legs around my waist.

"I really need this," Londa whispered into my ear and I moved in and out of her with a passion and fire that rocked us both. I didn't realize how hungry I was. Because Londa was throwing it back at me so good, I grabbed her soft, round ass and rode her to an explosive climax. She came so loudly beneath me, I felt like I was in love or something close to it.

So much for platonic relationships, I thought.

CHAPTER 18

The next morning I found myself making a tropical tango smoothie when Londa came into the kitchen. She wore her long white, wide legged linen pants with a white halter top. I wore a gray tee shirt and matching shorts. "Good morning," I called over my shoulder as she sat down at the kitchen table. She mumbled something in reply. The silence between us forced me to return to what I was doing. I mixed and diced mango, pineapple chunks, non-fat vanilla soy milk, a tablespoon of honey and some ice cubes. Then I put everything in the blender.

"Would you like to talk?" Londa asked from behind. "About what happened last night?"

I turned to face her and nodded. I even turned off the blender to give her my full attention.

"First of all, no regrets on my part, Choice," Londa began. "What happened, happened and I am not sorry or embarrassed about it. You're still my friend, my good friend and I hope that I haven't done anything to ruin our friendship."

I nodded.

"I don't think it should happen again," Londa went on, "not because it wasn't enjoyable." She smiled. "It was great."

I smiled back. Just the thought of what we had experienced together made me warm and hungry for an encore performance.

"But if we keep doing that, I'm afraid our friendship would go right out the window. Do you agree with me? This won't work unless you agree." She looked scared. "Because if you don't agree—"

I coughed, and then found my voice. "Yes, I agree. I treasure our friendship too much to jeopardize it."

Londa's voice softened with relief. "I've always looked at you as a big brother." That made me feel weird, as if what we had done was incestuous. "I like talking to you, getting the male perspective on things. What's the male perspective on what we did last night?"

"It can't happen again."

"I agree."

"And not because I wouldn't want it to."

Londa smiled sheepishly. "I feel that you're saying that to make me feel comfortable. Perhaps less guilty. After all, I *was* the aggressor."

A picture of Londa nude on the sundeck with her back toward me flashed through my mind. "You didn't do anything I didn't want you to do."

"You were very cooperative," Londa told me, and then smiled shyly.

Keep it light and talk it out, I told myself. "I expect you to go on with your life and I'm going to go on with mine."

"You won't be a stranger to me now?"

"No, Londa, there's no reason for that. We're friends, we'll always be friends."

Londa emitted a loud sigh of relief, "I'm glad to hear that."

I turned back to the blender and flipped the on switch. Its loud sound overpowered my thinking, breaking the uncomfortable silence between us.

Terry B.

CHAPTER 19

I left Los Angeles as happy as I was when I first arrived. My flight back to the East Coast was uneventful and gave me a lot of time to think. Summer was traditionally bad for me, but I tried to convince myself that this summer of 2000 would be different. I promised I would keep my career on track and do all the good work I knew I was capable of.

When I finally got to Newark International Airport, I was still filled with good vibes and determination. But when I got my luggage off the carousel the air around me suddenly changed. It wasn't something loud announced with blaring trumpets and cymbals. It was more like a sudden breeze on an oppressively hot day; it was welcomed, but totally unexpected. I was glad that I had my Nikon with me, sitting in the middle of my chest, hanging from a long black leather strap.

Men turned their heads and women whispered slyly. The ones who caused all of this commotion seemed oblivious; they were so much into each other that no one else mattered. Once you saw them you had to look twice. It was like seeing Venus and Serena Williams, the tennis pros, suddenly appear out of nowhere. You had to look because you might never see them in person again.

I stepped back, trying to bury myself in the crowd as I took my shots. I didn't want them to pose, and I definitely didn't want them to notice me. The shock of seeing them together did crazy things to my stomach. I felt like a kid getting ready for his first kiss and not sure how to position his nose as he went for the lips.

I knew that I would see them together eventually. I just didn't think it would be this soon. Right there in the airport: Lorrie Cunningham and Debrena Allen.

Debrena was probably coming from some trip and Lorrie was there to drive her home. They were smiling at each other and laughing, oblivious to the people that stared at them, including me.

Debrena was dark and Lorrie was light, dressed to thrill in the latest fashions, looking more like models than professional dancers. Nothing fancy on either of them, but their liveliness and wholesome beauty made them extremely provocative and sensual. Their very presence changed the atmosphere.

They chatted as they waited for Debrena's luggage to appear on the carousel, and when they saw it, they both grabbed for it at the same time. This resulted in Debrena almost losing her balance. Of course, this was another occasion for laughter. And of course, I had to capture that precious moment with my camera.

Am I ever going to get over this woman? I asked myself as I lowered my camera. It wasn't just about sex, which had been great. What got me and refused to let go was her personality and the fact that she loved her art as much as I loved mine. We made passionate love last summer, but we also talked and shared our dreams and visions. I had never gone to that level with any other woman. I had deep conversations with Londa, but with Debrena the conversations were tied up with sweet sensuality and I was hooked. She became a drug and the more she withdrew from me the more I had to have her.

The only thing that kept me from going completely crazy that summer was the fact that she let me down easy. When I realized that it was over I had gotten to the point where, although hurting, I could walk away like a man. I knew there was no way I could have her if it wasn't what she wanted. To her credit, she had never deceived me like that.

I suddenly became angry as I watched them together; knowing that Lorrie was getting something I once felt belonged only to me. I never got an opportunity to work something out with Debrena. As crazy as it seemed I was willing to share Debrena, not with another man, but with another woman. I cursed myself as Lorrie led Debrena out of the airport.

CHAPTER 20

We were in the downstairs conference room, my favorite meeting place at NTA. They were all there: my set designer, Princess Slade, hair dresser, Karen Jackson, and my assistant, Lyedecker. Lorrie was sitting off to the side.

Her hair was shorter than it was last summer because she had taken out her extensions. She had it parted in the middle and curled under, emphasizing her long face and classic cheekbones. Her eyebrows were thick and her lashes naturally long over light brown eyes. Her nose was long and her full lips were painted pink. She could've passed for a model with the outfit she wore that morning: a collared button-up shirt with a man's style pin-striped blazer and matching skirt that had side drawstrings. On her feet she wore black pumps with black bows and a black leather necklace hung around her neck.

Because I didn't want to get caught staring I began the meeting. "I hate early meetings, so you know if we're here this early, it must be very important."

It wasn't really that early, 10 A.M., but none of us were early risers.

"I'm just glad you didn't call me at five in the morning like you did last time," Karen said.

I smiled, somewhat embarrassed. "You all know each other,

but you may not know the young woman sitting at the end of the table. Her name is Lorrie Cunningham."

Lorrie said hi and everyone echoed her. After they all introduced themselves I stated the obvious. "Lorrie will be doing makeup as part of the team." I let that sink in. "We have a two day prep on this one. Princess, you want to tell us who we'll be working with?"

Princess moved her blonde hair behind her ear and got into professional mode.

She taught theatre at Union County College and was involved in a theatre workshop this summer, teaching a group of children every aspect of theatre production. She was a "touchy feely" person and I had adjusted to her happy hands. She also had two babies, her dogs, a Rottweiler and a Cocker Spaniel.

I recalled a crazy conversation she had with Karen sometime last summer when we all first worked together.

It was that eternal question that all Black women asked Black men, but would never ask White women: Why are so many Black men attracted to White women? It was only because Princess was so cool that Karen had the nerve to ask her. Although she had never dated any Black men, Princess tried to answer. She had seen Spike Lee's *Jungle Fever* and felt she had a worthwhile opinion. Of course, Karen verbally batted away any rationale that Princess could come up with. Karen was convinced that it was all a "dick thing" for Black men, and had nothing to do with the sex appeal of White women.

As Karen saw it, Black men could never love a White woman because all White women had flat behinds. Princess reached behind and grabbed two handfuls of her own behind. Karen laughed so hard that tears came to her eyes. Princess joined in on the laughter. As a result, they grew to admire each other's work ethic and to respect each other's talents.

"Three beautiful girls," Princess told us, and then sent three photos around the table. "They've been with Bethann for a little while, but this is the first time we've used them and this is their first major shoot."

I was the last one to get the head shots. They were all beautiful Black women, various shades of brown. I immediately thought of some type of pyramid configuration, but I didn't want to think too much about the shoot; I didn't want to lock myself into anything. I wanted to brainstorm with my crew and let the creativity flow.

Princess had gone through at least a hundred photos to find these girls. But I knew it didn't stop there. She had interviewed each model to find out what their goals were beyond the brief time they would spend in my loft. "Thank you, Princess."

"Karen went down to the agency with me," Princess said. "She was there when I interviewed the girls." The interviews were the equivalent of an audition because Princess saw every shoot as a theatrical event. The models became actresses on the set she conceived and put together as the stylist for the project.

"The hair will be together," Karen said. "By the way, your hair looks great."

I smiled modestly at the compliment. Her short Halle Berry cut wasn't bad either.

CHAPTER 21

Karen was a serious hair professional, specializing in braiding and weaving. At age nine she started as a receptionist at her mother's salon and had her own chair at age fifteen. At age twenty-two she opened her own salon, Jackson Hair Designs, in the Port section of Elizabeth, New Jersey on First Street, two blocks from the Pioneer Homes housing project. She now lived uptown, but never forgot her roots and was always more than willing to give back.

I met her when I decided to grow dreadlocks. She got me started the right way. I had heard too many stories about brothers who had their hair locked and found their hair breaking off, making their natural experiment a living nightmare. I started out with baby dreds in the summer of 1999, and now had healthy locks down to my shoulders thanks to Karen's incomparable skills.

Because she liked numbers as much as Dany, I told her how much money she was going to make for a one day shoot. "Who do I have to kill for that kind of money?" she asked, and then smiled.

"What will you do with the hair?" Lorrie asked much to my surprise. I figured since this was Lorrie's first time with us, she would just sit and take everything in.

Karen smiled broadly, glad to talk about her favorite subject:

hair. "Excuse me," she said to Lyedecker, snatching the photos away from him; he was drooling over the pictures. Holding up the photo of model number one, she said, "They all like long hair, but I don't want them to look the same. For this lady, I'm going with a layered cut, with sewn in hair enhancements. After I layer it, all she has to do is wrap it the night before, then let it out the day of the shoot."

Lorrie looked at her, fascinated by the process. "How will you keep it from drying out?"

"I'll tell her to keep her hair hydrated with a hot oil treatment and leave it in conditioner. I like Paul Mitchell hair products."

"For my second lady here," Karen said, holding up the picture of model number two. "I'll go with a bone straight look with bright red streaks in it. I'll use a flat iron and hot-red highlights that I'll create by adding hair extensions through the front of her hair."

"Sounds good to me," Lorrie said enthusiastically.

"For my third model, I'll braid her hair in thick plaits, going straight back from her hairline and trailing down her back. I'll even add some blonde highlights, using hair extensions."

"Sounds good," Lorrie said.

"Excuse me," Lyedecker said as he reached across Karen to retrieve the photos.

"We work so hard and all he does is look at pictures," Princess said to Lorrie. They all smiled at each other and I stood at the front of the table like a proud father.

"Where will the clothes be coming from?" Lorrie asked.

"Would you like to see them?" Princess asked and I was somewhat surprised because she usually didn't bring out the clothes until the last minute. "Lyedecker, would you please make yourself useful?"

When Lyedecker left the room, Princess told Lorrie, "Karen helped me pull the outfits together. I have a lot more than we'll be able to use, but the variety is truly impressive." The gentle giant wheeled in the clothes. "These are from Otomix, Farmon, Formula One, and Hot Skins, hot stuff for personal trainers or anyone who likes to look fashionable in athletic clothes."

There were ohs and ahs at the fashion parade of drawstring cropped pants, shorts trimmed with satin, baby tees, cotton ribbed tie dyed outfits, cotton velour track suits, jumpsuits, and cotton twill pants.

"*Urban Vibe* magazine wants to showcase some summer fashions for the sexy female athlete," Karen told Lorrie who held onto a bleached, sand color cami tank top and matching sport shorts like she didn't want to let them go.

"Dag, girls," Lorrie exclaimed. "I'm going to have to come correct with the makeup to complement these fierce outfits."

"What do you think you'll do?" Karen asked. "I've seen too many women with great hair and wack makeup."

Lorrie smiled, "I know what you mean, girl. I think I'll go with a natural look. Just a little mascara, blush, and lip gloss. I like to add blush around the corner of the eyes; it lightens up the whole face. I prefer MAC products."

Karen and Princess nodded approvingly. Any doubts I had about Lorrie fitting in were dispelled. Even Lyedecker seemed pleased, but he was a sucker for a beautiful face.

I didn't realize that I was staring until Princess got right into my face and called my name.

"Yes, Princess," I said, looking away from Lorrie.

"I said, do you think we're ready to go? To do the shoot?"

"Yeah," I said weakly. "Yeah, we're ready. I'm meeting with Carrie right after we finish in here. I'll let her know we're ready to go. Look everybody, that's all I wanted to share. We're finished for now."

As I moved to get past Princess she whispered, "I can't believe you didn't hear me calling you."

"I hear you loud and clear now," I whispered back, a tone of dismissal in my voice.

"Must be jet lag," Princess commented as she walked away from me.

I was the first one out of the conference room.

CHAPTER 22

I found Carrie Nelson in her spacious office, pulling on the jacket to her dark blue suit over a white silk blouse. She stopped with her jacket halfway up when she saw me.

"Am I late?" Carrie asked.

"No," I said. "I'm a little early."

"Early is always better." I helped her into her jacket. "Such a gentleman."

I blushed, touched by the compliment from this sweet smelling, silver gray haired, elegant lady. She gave a pretty good idea what Dany, her daughter, would look like in middle age. At age fifty-eight, Carrie Nelson was strong, athletic, and inspirational, with her trim physique and razor sharp business mind. She was about five-four and ate a lot of fruit and vegetables, whole wheat bread, chicken, salmon, and beans. I knew because I had been invited to her home for many meals.

I followed her out of her office and down the hall to the large conference room, with the long stained walnut oak table and the white walls that served as screens for her power point presentations. I pulled a chair out for her at the head of the table. Then I adjusted the blinds so that the bright sun wouldn't cook us.

"So considerate," Carrie remarked as I sat at the far end of the table. She smiled at me like I was a favorite nephew.

"Will Curtis and Dany be joining us?"

"They're both doing big things outside the office," Carrie informed me. "I thought that you and I should spend this time together."

Her skin was stretched so tightly over her face that I suspected some minor plastic surgery. Diet and exercise didn't take care of everything.

"Is there an agenda? Did you want to see me for a specific reason?"

She went on like she hadn't heard me. "How was your vacation, Choice? Dany told me that you recently spent some time in L.A."

I blushed. "I visited a friend."

"I like L.A., but it's a little too warm for me this time of year," Carrie said, looking down at the diamonds on her fingers and wrists, then back up at me. "The last time I was there on business, Dany and I dined at The Firehouse. The portions are huge, really too much for me, but the food was delicious. I love their ground turkey patty, without the bun of course."

"I've never been there."

After a moment of silence, Carrie asked, "Do you think Curtis is happy at NTA?"

I paused. "Curtis hasn't expressed any dissatisfaction to me."

She stared at me intensely. "Sometimes I get the impression that he doesn't like taking orders from two women."

"Well, he's never said anything to me."

Carrie winked. "I wouldn't expect you to tell me if he wasn't happy here. I don't pay you to spy on your friends." I was glad when she changed the subject. "I'm so happy that you have all the people you need for the *Urban Vibe* photo shoot." Then she got down to why she wanted to meet with me: she wanted me to do a favor for one of her friends. "Although I know you'd rather do fine art photography rather than commercial photography."

I flashbacked to the last time she asked me to do a favor for her: a thirteen month calendar shoot for the Dominique St. Claire Dance Studio for a fundraiser. It was when I met Debrena and Lorrie.

"Cee Cee Martin is a wonderful designer. She does hand-crafted knitwear designs, nothing for an old lady like me, but they would look great on my daughter."

"Are these photos for a catalog?"

"It's a live show, a fashion showcase at Malika's Place."

I didn't feel the need to tell her that I had been there with Curtis.

"Cee Cee has opened a new store uptown, and this show is her way of reaching out to the public. Because her parents are dear friends of mine, I offered to arrange some great shots for her, for publicity or whatever. She saw the calendar you did for Dominique's fundraiser and was very impressed. 'I have to have that photographer,' she said to me. Very excited, I might add. Would you be a dear and take some shots?"

Of course there was no way that I could say no.

CHAPTER 23

When I came out of my meeting with Carrie I ran into Curtis. "Looking for you yesterday, and here you are today," Curtis said.

I cursed my bad luck because he was the last person I wanted to see that morning.

"Hard to let go of that good thing?" Curtis asked as I tried to avoid his smiling eyes. "I told you it would happen."

"Nothing happened," I said a little too loudly.

"You sly dog, you can't play a player. Did she call out your name? Did she scratch your back? Is she a freak, or what?"

"Man, get outta my face," I said as I pushed pass Curtis.

"Don't be like that, Choice," he said, hot on my heels.

"I didn't tell you anything went down," I called out over my shoulder.

Curtis laughed loudly. "You don't have to tell me, Brother Man. It's written all over your face."

I stopped.

"Choice, man, this is Curtis. I mean what happened was bound to happen."

"I didn't say anything."

"You are two consenting adults. What y'all do is what y'all do."

"I just don't want you thinking that Londa is some hot in the ass trick."

"Brother Man, you never gave me the impression Londa was anything but a fine upstanding young woman."

I couldn't shake the feeling that Curtis was making fun of me, but he maintained a straight face so I couldn't tear into him like I wanted to. "It happened," I confessed. "But I don't expect it to happen again."

Curtis waited.

"It was an accident." I said.

"Like a car crash?"

"No. Not like that. More like…we both had a need, and we helped each other out."

"Who could argue with that?"

"It wasn't anything we planned."

Curtis nodded.

"I don't want to hear about this from anyone else. I don't want my sex life to be the subject of office gossip."

Curtis touched his chest near his heart. "It hurts when you play me cheap like that. You my man. I'm glad you got yours off. So how was it? I know it was good."

I felt real uncomfortable talking to Curtis about Londa, but I didn't know how to change the subject without sounding like some chump that was less than a man. "It was good, we enjoyed each other."

"I bet you were in that all weekend."

"Not all weekend."

Curtis smiled, "You animal." He pulled something out of his pants pocket. "I think this belongs to you."

I took the spare key to my loft from Curtis and quickly walked ahead of him on my way out of the building. With his long legs it was hard for me to shake him.

"What brings you by this early in the morning anyway?" Curtis asked as we walked the corridors of NTA.

"I had to meet with my people. I got that *Urban Vibe* shoot coming up in a few days."

"Well," Curtis said as he stood near the staircase that led up to his second floor office, "welcome back. Things were a little dull around here without you."

I walked down the hall and felt his eyes on me. I turned and found Curtis staring at me. I thought he was going to say something, but all he did was smile. I did not like that smile.

CHAPTER 24

When I stepped outside of the NTA building I noticed Princess. She didn't see me as she reached into her back pocket and pulled out a pack of cigarettes.

"I thought you stopped that."

Princess turned to me. "Fifty kids in a six week summer program," she told me, like that explained it all. Finding a lighter in her front pocket, she lit up. When she blew out the white fog, she looked more relaxed.

"I really like Lorrie. I hope she works with us more often."

I didn't expect to hear that come from Princess. She had only known Lorrie for about thirty minutes give or take. I didn't know how to respond so I said what I thought she wanted to hear, "We'll see. I have to get something out of my ride."

Princess just waived me off and continued smoking.

Last summer, while I was lying in bed with Debrena, I heard on a talk show that sometimes a person comes to hate the thing they love. Dr. Joy Browne, the radio psychologist, was talking about artists and how sometimes they self-destruct. They can no longer find their muse and, consequently, find themselves hating their art. I didn't want to listen to her expound on the subject, but Debrena was somewhat of a radio talk show fan. If I listened to any radio station it was further down the dial, WWRL, which featured the great DJ and talk show host Bob Law who played classic R&B.

Dr. Browne went on about how artists become obsessed with their art to the point that all they know *is* their art. Eventually anything that doesn't have to do with art is of no importance to them including family, friends, and lovers.

As I sat behind the steering wheel I wondered what my life would be like without photography. Perhaps I could be a regular person, someone who worked nine to five and didn't allow their passions to consume them. But all I knew was photography. I pulled out my date book to add Carrie's special project to my schedule when I caught some movement at the front of the NTA building.

It was Lorrie and she was talking on her cell phone. She had taken off her jacket and looked extremely relaxed. I couldn't imagine why she'd still be there. Then I looked around and realized that Princess's and Karen's cars were parked in the lot. On the one hand it was good because I could solicit some help for Carrie's special project, but on the other hand it would mean another encounter with Lorrie. I watched Lorrie standing long and tall and snapped her picture. Her phone call was brief, but instead of reentering the building, she stood there like she was waiting for someone.

My plan was to stay in my ride until Lorrie went back into the building, and then I would walk to the building to talk briefly with my crew. I knew that Lyedecker would be there for a full work day, but I also knew that Princess and Karen could disappear at any moment to follow their own agenda; if I missed them here I might not be able to catch up with them later. I didn't need a full crew or even a crew at all, but I did want either Princess or Karen to accompany me. This way I would have something to take my mind off the fact that I hated covering fashion shows. I didn't like the crowds or the amateur photographers that seemed to get in the way as they snapped pictures of sisters and mothers, daughters and lovers.

Suddenly, Lorrie broke into a smile as a sea green Lexus

pulled up to the curb in front of her. Because of the tinted windows I couldn't see who was in the car.

Debrena stepped out of the Lexus, looking like a diva as usual and my stomach did a flip flop that made me dizzy. She handed Lorrie a black makeup case that was half the size of a small briefcase. Lorrie gave Debrena a tight hug.

With Lorrie still in her arms, Debrena moved in to claim Lorrie's lips. If there was any surprise on Lorrie's part I didn't notice it. They were so into each other that they didn't even bother to look around to see if anybody was watching. I captured their big kiss on camera.

What are you doing? I asked myself. My heart was beating like drums of passion as Lorrie turned and went back into the building with her makeup case under her arm.

Was I letting my passion destroy me like my father let his passion for my mother destroy them both? I wondered as I lowered my camera.

I began to sweat as Debrena drove toward me, and our eyes met for a brief moment.

CHAPTER 25

Lorrie

I walked back into the conference room. Princess and Karen smiled at me. I had let them talk me into doing their makeovers.

"Where's the guy?" I asked as I put my makeup case on the long table.

Princess laughed out loud. "Lyedecker ran as soon as you left to make your phone call."

"He didn't want to get caught up in this, as he called it, 'woman's stuff'," Karen explained.

"Do you have anything in that case for me?" Princess asked, and I knew what she meant.

"You mean do I have anything in here for White women?" I laughed as Princess blushed bright red. To keep things light I said, "I have some Bobbi Brown makeup in here, which should take care of you."

Princess beamed.

"Me first," Karen said, sitting herself firmly in a chair beside me.

"That's okay with you?" I asked Princess.

"We worked that out while you were making your call," Princess told me. "Karen has to get back to her shop. I'm a little more flexible, no kids today."

They were real comfortable with each other and that made me even more relaxed. I hadn't expected to spend so much time at NTA that morning, but after Choice's brief meeting the conversation flowed so well and was so wide ranging that I found myself reluctant to leave.

Before I could begin on Karen's face, Choice came back into the room. His face was shiny with sweat and he looked uncomfortable. *Does he want to speak only to Princess and Karen?* I asked myself. *Have I overstayed my welcome?*

"I don't want to interrupt," Choice began, and Karen turned to face him.

"Well, don't," Karen said jokingly. "Lorrie is about to make me more beautiful than I already am."

"Me too," Princess chimed in.

"That's nice," Choice said, his face neutral. Standing in the doorway, he was not the man he was earlier that morning.

"Can we help you with something?" Karen asked. "I can't wait to walk into the shop with my new face. The girls are just going to die."

"They'll probably think you went to the Maybelline counter at the mall," Princess added.

"I do like Maybelline's pressed powder and concealer," Karen admitted.

"But this will be a hundred times better," I said.

"Before you get into all that," Choice said. "I just want to say that Carrie has me on a special project. Princess? Karen? Can either or both of you help me out?"

"Is this special project going to delay the *Urban Vibe* shoot?" Karen asked with concern. "Choice, I've juggled so much to do this."

"The *Urban Vibe* shoot is on schedule," Choice told her. "The special project I'm talking about is tomorrow night."

"So soon, Choice?" Princess asked.

"I'm doing a favor for a friend of Carrie's," Choice told them.

"Like that calendar for that dance studio last summer?" Karen asked, and I felt a pang of anxiety.

"You handled that all by yourself, and it turned out great," Princess reminded him.

I closely watched Choice's facial expression. Now that I had met Karen and Princess I really wanted to work on the *Urban Vibe* project.

A small smile crept across Choice's face. "What you're saying is that if I could handle the calendar by myself I should be able to handle this special project by myself?"

"He's a brilliant man," Princess said as she lightly patted Choice on his broad back. "Isn't he a brilliant man, Karen?"

"Brilliant and cute too," Karen added.

"I guess that means no?" Choice asked.

"I have hair appointments from noon to midnight," Karen told him.

"I have a family gathering to attend tomorrow night," Princess said. "Sorry."

He looked at me, but I didn't expect any consideration. Besides I had promised that I would do Debrena's makeup for a fashion showcase she had tomorrow evening.

"What does Miss Carrie want you to do this time?" Karen asked.

"A fashion show for Cee Cee Designs."

My heart fell like a stone down into my stomach.

"Cee Cee has some nice stuff," Karen said. "Some of my customers like her stuff. But you have to have a damn near perfect figure to make that stuff fit right. Knitwear doesn't lie on a body. You either have the goods or you don't."

A body like Debrena's, I thought.

"I'll see you later," Choice said as he stepped out into the hall.

"Let's get it on, make me beautiful," Karen said as she turned back toward me.

"Excuse me for a minute," I told Karen before I went off to catch Choice. In the hallway I called out to him. He turned like he was surprised to see me. He stood still like a statue as I walked quickly toward him.

"Yes, Lorrie?"

"About the fashion show tomorrow night—"

"No offense, but I can't use you."

"I just wanted you to know—"

"What I mean is that it's going to be hectic there, and I'll be one among many photographers," Choice told me. "I think you're good, real good, but you don't have the experience that Karen and Princess have. When they work with me on outside shoots they have to do a whole lot of things. I couldn't throw you into all of that. That's a baptism by fire that you don't need. Trust me."

I was dismissed.

CHAPTER 26

As it turned out, I made out better doing the special project by myself. The show was supposed to start at 8:00 P.M., but when I walked into Malika's Place at 8:30 there was no indication that I had missed anything. A long runway extended from a small stage in the back of the club and everyone was making happy trips back and forth to the buffet table. Because I had my laminated NTA press pass hanging from my neck, along with my camera, and equipment shoulder bag I got into the restaurant without paying admission. The people at the door told me to make myself at home, which I figured to mean get my grub on, but I wasn't interested in food. All I wanted to do was take my shots and get out of there. I had planned to shoot fifteen rolls of film and I thought that was more than enough.

On a table I found a discarded program. The three major segments were Sexy Wear, Swim Wear, and Off The Hook Wear. I saw some amateur photographers who were obviously family members or friends with disposable cameras. From unseen speakers someone played "I Wish" by Carl Thomas over and over again until I got sick of it. When I looked at my watch I discovered that it was almost 9:00 P.M. Just when I thought I couldn't take anymore, the show began. The crowd of about three hundred, mostly Black women, took their seats at small white linen covered tables as the lights became dim around the runway.

The Announcer came out dressed flamboyantly in a black and purple outfit. He was loud and gay, but I didn't hold that against him. "Cee Cee's designs are for the *bold* and the *beautiful*," he told us in an overly dramatic voice. "She wants to make all women feel *gorgeous!*"

I raised my camera with the sound of the Announcer's voice ringing in my ears. I couldn't wait to shoot and split.

"Be *bold*, be *beautiful*. Soon Cee Cee's designs will be available from coast to coast, at Nordstorm's and Traffic stores in Southern California, Detroit, Chicago, Atlanta, New York, Houston, and Virginia Beach. But because Cee Cee was born right here in Elizabeth, New Jersey, she is sharing her fabulous collection with her friends first."

There was scattered applause. I, for one, just wanted to see the outfits so that most of my work for that evening would be done. The first segment began with the music of Aaliyah, a new singer I had some respect for.

"*Sweet Mya* is looking even sweeter in a two-toned pink, two piece outfit with halter top," the Announcer said as the petite model came down the runway. I snapped off some quick shoots then faded off to the side, out of the crowd's view. "*Vibrant* and *exciting* in handcrafted knitwear, only for the *bold* and the *beautiful!*"

After the model strutted her stuff and disappeared behind the stage, another model came out. "*Monica, Monica, Monica*, sexy *Monica. Delicious* in a bright and bold, long, gold skirt and lime green, orange, turquoise top. Accentuating her full figure."

Pree-ty Toni," the Announcer said even before the model came out onto the runway. "*Vi-va-ci-ous* in drawstring pants and a multi colored top. *Pree-ty Toni* you are looking very pretty this summer evening. *Strut* your stuff for the people who know *what time it is!*"

I got my shots of the models coming and going. The tempo of the music picked up with Aaliyah singing "Try Again." Then Debrena Allen came out and I almost fell to the floor.

"A very special guest model," the Announcer said as the

crowd went wild with their applause. *"De-vas-stat-ting Debrena,* you've seen her in music videos, a perfect vision of loveliness in a hooded, deep purple ensemble, a short one piece knit that hugs all that you want to *hug!"*

Our eyes met just before I raised my camera. Then I moved in to shoot her, and she held a straight face, all business. Because there was no escaping this scene I went ahead and snapped three quick shots. On her way back up the runway I snapped three more shots.

Then it was the Swim Wear segment. Debrena was the first one out. She wore a red knitted jacket over a matching halter string bikini.

The background music was the "Thong Song" by Sisqo.

Monica, Mya, and Toni came out in equally revealing knit wear, but I only had eyes for Debrena. I became jealous at all the attention that she was getting from the crowd, jealous because she was revealing what I once thought was only for me. She turned her back to the front crowd, with her head pointed over her shoulder, and dropped her red knitted jacket.

The crowd went wild because the bottom of her bikini was nothing but a cup of knit in the front and a string between her cheeks in the back. Her perfect pear shaped ass was prominently displayed for all to see. Everybody rose to their feet, clapping and stomping like they were witnessing the second coming of Michael Jordan. I snapped my photos, recording the model and the pandemonium that she created. Monica, Mya, and Toni joined her, making a tight circle on the runway, all beautiful Black women, displaying their assets.

That was when someone yelled, "Oh, hell no!" And it wasn't the Announcer.

"Hell, no!" the man said again, and before the two muscular bouncers at the entrance to Malika's Place could grab him, he was running toward the runway. "Toni, Toni," he called out as he ran. People started screaming and another man jumped in front of him to block his way. The angry man threw a punch and the models on the stage began to scream; that is, every one but Debrena, who was stretching her neck to see what was going on. Without even thinking about it I jumped onto the stage. Much later, I would tell myself that I jumped onstage to protect the models from the chairs that began to fly across the room. But at that moment all I knew was that I was onstage with my arms outstretched and shielding Debrena from harm.

The club broke into two camps: those who were down with the man that rushed toward Toni on the stage and the others who were trying to help the bouncers regain some order.

A small group of the models stood behind me as I backed up down the runway. The man that had come for Toni disappeared in a mountain of bodies that looked like a football pileup. Before I knew it I was being pushed out of a backstage exit that lead to the parking lot behind the restaurant. I fought to push my way back into the club, but it was a losing battle. I wanted to make sure Debrena was okay, but that was a mission impossible. As I walked to my ride I heard the distant sound of police sirens.

CHAPTER 27

I got into my ride and drove around to the front of Malika's Place. By that time the police were on the scene and escorting people out of the restaurant. Although there were four police cars at the front of the restaurant, I didn't see the police put anybody into one. They seemed intent upon getting everybody out of the restaurant and away from the scene of the near riot.

Debrena came through the crowd, dressed in a tan summer trench coat and carrying a large canvas tote bag. The police directed her to the side of the club and she walked about a block down. I thought she was looking for her parked car, but the way she walked and all that she carried gave me the impression that she wasn't driving that evening.

I drove beside Debrena and blew my horn. She looked over at me as I lowered my window. "Need a ride?"

Debrena nodded and walked toward me as I pulled to a stop. I pushed the door open as she ran around to the passenger side. She got in and slammed the door behind her. "I'm glad I ran into you."

"What happened to your car?" I asked as I pulled out into the traffic.

"In the shop," Debrena said as she tied the belt of her trench coat around her small waist. "Some problem with the alternator, or at least that's what they told me. I never trust those guys. My

Dad always tells me to bring a man with me when I take my car to the shop; sometimes a man is hard to find."

I looked over at Debrena and couldn't tell if she were joking or not.

"I got a ride to Malika's with Toni. I was supposed to get a ride back with her, but it was her jealous ass boyfriend that rushed the stage."

"What was that all about?"

"He didn't want her to be in the fashion showcase, especially in some of those skimpy outfits. She thought she could walk out without him saying anything."

I nodded. "I was really surprised to see you up there."

"A favor for a friend."

"That's how I got there, doing a favor for the head of NTA."

Debrena chuckled softly. "When you saw me, you looked so stunned, so shocked."

"I had no idea you'd be in that show."

"Lorrie tried to tell you."

"I don't think so," I said, suddenly angry.

"She tried, Choice," Debrena said raising her voice. "Lorrie said you kept going on about her not being ready to help you at Malika's."

I stared at the road.

"But you were glad to see me," The way she said it made it more of a statement than a question.

"How can you say that?" I hissed.

"I want to know, Choice."

I wanted to be tough, but I felt like the weakest punk. I had dreamt about running into her, but none of the scenarios were like this. "You've moved on, Debrena. I've moved on. We had a hot summer together. Let's just leave it at that."

"I would if you didn't look at me like you wanted to tongue me down."

I blushed. "Am I that obvious?"

"I'm afraid so, but I find it flattering."

"The attraction was strong from the beginning, you know that."

Debrena nodded. After a moment of silence, she added, "I'm glad I ran into you. And not just for a ride home. The way things ended between us was rather abrupt. I never wanted you to hate me."

"Should I hate you? For leaving me for Lorrie?"

"Look, Choice, I didn't leave you for anybody. What we had just ran its course. Like you said, it was time to move on. For me and you."

"And Lorrie had nothing to do with it?"

"Lorrie has been my friend since we were ten years old; I never thought she'd be my lover."

"So it was Lorrie's idea?"

"It was something that happened. Nothing I'm ashamed of and nothing I have to make excuses for. I know you want to see Lorrie as some wild lesbian that seduced poor, innocent me. That's not the way it went down. I love Lorrie."

The way Debrena put it out there I had to accept it. She didn't need me to rescue her, and it was obvious that she was more than happy with Lorrie. It wasn't the way I wanted it, but there was nothing I could do about it. I pulled into the street where Debrena lived and parked in front of her house.

She leaned over and kissed me softly on my cheek. "Thanks for the ride. Maybe I'll see you around."

"I don't want to leave that to chance," I told her, and she looked at me strangely.

"Are you hitting on me, Choice Fowler?"

"After all that we've been through, all that we've meant to each other, hitting on you seems a little lame."

"Whatever you call it, however you say it, you want me in your bed."

"Or in your bed."

"That's something that I'll have to think about," Debrena told me as she pushed the door open. "I'll call you."

I watched as she walked up the cobble-stoned walk to her house. I didn't pull off until she disappeared. Then I drove into the dark night.

CHAPTER 28

For the last shot of the *Urban Vibe* set I had the three models stand together in a geometric shape: one model up front and the other two to her left and right, forming a human wedge. I had them stare at me with a look that said, *wouldn't you like to come out and play?* Because I knew that *Urban Vibe* magazine's readership was primarily young Black men, I wanted the photo spread to be sexy but not obvious. I didn't want to exploit the women, but I wanted the young men to get the impression that these beautiful women were more than willing to be a part of their fantasies. I wanted the men who flipped through the pages of *Urban Vibe* to get the sense that they were walking through a park and just happened to come across these three beauties in their stylish athletic clothes: baby tees, drawstring pants, and short shorts. The colors were just right: black with red, heather grey with red, soft colors like pink, lilac, light blue, and white, that made the models look athletic, but still very feminine.

Lyedecker loaded my cameras, a Nikon F4 with an 80-20mm zoom lens and a Bronica SQ with a 40 mm lens. As my personal assistant he even handled my music, putting on the Blackbyrds, a pop/jazz group founded by Dr. Donald Byrd when he was the head of the music department at Howard University. On the tape were many of their well known hits like "Do It Fluid" and "Rock Creek Park," along with some instrumentals that really energized me and the models.

Princess had done a great job on the set, even bringing in

some grass pads to serve as a floor for the shoot. In the background she set up a backdrop that pictured a blue sky above a park, complete with a park bench. I stopped asking Princess where she got her props. As a long time stage manager for many local groups I knew she had some serious contacts. If there was anything she felt she needed she could easily get her hands on it.

Karen did the hair of the models the night before, so there was no reason for her to be at the shoot, but she was there, making sure everything looked all right and checking to see if the models needed some extra touches.

The person who had the most work, and the one I was somewhat worried about, was Lorrie. She had come in early, to meet the models and apply their makeup. My fear for Lorrie was that she would get overwhelmed and not have the models ready for me. She came in early and went right to work. She had met the models before with Karen so she knew who she was working with and what would make each of the models look their best.

I noticed that she used M.A.C. products, brushes, and pencils. She used blush around the corners of the model's eyes to lighten their faces, along with lip gloss to enhance their big bright smiles. I was pleased with Lorrie's work because she gave the models the feeling that they were being treated extra special and that made them eager to do anything I asked of them.

All and all, the *Urban Vibe* shoot went great and I was really proud of my crew.

As they made their way out of my loft, I couldn't help but look over at Lorrie. Common sense told me to go over to her to compliment her on her work, but I didn't. I had no doubt in my mind that she and Debrena had talked about what happened at Malika's Place and about the upcoming *Urban Vibe* shoot. I would've given anything to be a fly on the wall during that conversation. But all that amounted to nothing. Lorrie had come through with flying colors, and there was nothing I could complain about. Still, as I looked at her talking with Karen and Princess, while walking out with them, I couldn't shake the feeling that she had taken something that belonged to me.

CHAPTER 29

Lorrie

After we made love, I sat on the edge of her bed and reached for my shirt on a nearby chair. My jeans was across the room, near the closed bedroom door. My bra and matching panties were draped over the doorknob. Debrena had talked me into doing a little strip tease and that was where I began. As I buttoned my blouse, I looked over my shoulder at her. She was naked, lying on her stomach. "You never did tell me about your project for NTA," she reminded me.

"What's to talk about?"

"Did you like it? Will you do it again? Was Choice mean to you?"

"Yes. Yes. And no."

"Smart ass," Debrena said, and then hit me in the back with a soft pillow.

I laughed. "I really enjoyed myself, D. Everything took place in Choice's loft and everybody was very professional. I worked real well with the models and I'd love to do it again. As for Choice being mean to me, why would he want to do that?"

"I told you he drove me home after the show, what I didn't tell you was that he hit on me."

I turned toward her, shifting on the bed so that I faced her. I got a tingle between my thighs as I looked upon her shapely ass. "Did you invite him in?"

"Don't be silly."

"I'm not being silly. Why didn't you tell me this before?"

"Because I didn't know how I wanted to deal with Choice's interest in me."

Unshed tears stung my eyes like someone had thrown sand in my face. "You told me that you and Choice were over, D. Over because you knew that you loved me, that you always loved me."

"Calm down, Lorrie."

I jumped up from the bed, ready to make a quick exit. I felt silly standing there naked from the waist down.

"I don't want you to go, Lorrie. There's no reason for you to walk out of here angry."

"If you want Choice—"

"Lorrie, it's not about me wanting Choice."

"But he hit on you."

"He and a million other men."

The thought of Debrena leaving me for Choice made me sick to my stomach and brought on a pounding headache. I was so tense that I felt like I had been dipped in hot water, and then frozen solid. I didn't want to have this conversation, but I made no move to put on my skirt. Instead, I sat back down on the bed next to Debrena.

"It's not about me going to bed with Choice. I'm not saying any of this to hurt you or make you feel insecure."

"We just made love, D. Forgive me if I'm feeling a little vulnerable right now."

"I understand vulnerability, Lorrie. I'm also vulnerable to you. You can't imagine how vulnerable I am." She looked at me like she wanted to cry. "Do you think I want Choice?"

"I think you like the idea of Choice wanting you, especially after all this time."

Debrena smiled a brilliant smile. "You know me too well."

"Everybody wants that, D. To be wanted, to be desired by someone they find desirable."

"Choice could never replace you."

"I'm glad to hear that," I said sarcastically as I stroked Debrena's bare back.

"What we have has been a long time coming."

"So why are we talking about this man?"

"Not just any man, Lorrie. I'm talking about Choice."

"Okay, Choice."

"Because after I had Choice, I didn't want any other man. The sex I had with Choice was so intense. I can't describe it."

I was embarrassed by the intensity of Debrena's remembrance. "You make it sound like it's something every woman should experience."

"At least once, Lorrie. At least once."

"I never had a man; I never wanted a man. I'm more than happy with our relationship. I've been with many other women, but I've never been this satisfied, this complete."

"I know, baby, I know."

"Then why do you keep talking about pleasure from this man? Like it's something I'm missing out on."

That was when Debrena turned to lay on her back. Her legs were slightly parted as I looked down on her. "It's just something I think you should experience," she said looking straight up at the high ceiling in her bedroom.

I was stunned, breathless, and speechless all at the same time. How could Debrena think I would go for something like that? I knew that I wanted Debrena to test me like Angela tested Marcy. Was this my test?

To avoid further conversation, I rested my head on Debrena's shoulder and stroked her between her breasts as I made my way down to her wide spread thighs.

CHAPTER 30

Choice

U nder the red light in the darkroom I listened to the music that I inherited from my parents. To the casual listener it was the best of classic R&B, but to me it was the background of my life story. These songs contained values that my parents taught me. Sometimes when I used this music in my darkroom or on a shoot, the memories of my parents were so intense that I had to leave the room to get myself together. But the best times were when the music just filled me up with its spirit and made me appreciate the creativity and soulfulness of its creators.

Whenever I would put on a CD for Debrena, she would call it "old timey music," but I never felt it was a put down. The music of sexy soul artists like Teddy Pendergrass, Al Green, Freddy Jackson, Luther Vandross, Eddie Kendricks, and the Isley Brothers provided the background for our intense lovemaking.

The last time I spoke to Debrena she told me she would call. That simple promise put me on Cloud Nine whenever I thought about it. My mother would always tell me not to count my chickens before they hatch, but I took Debrena at her word. I eagerly checked my voicemail for messages and even checked the phone to make sure that everything was working correctly. I could've called her, but it wouldn't be the same; I had to know that Debrena wanted me.

I was inside my darkroom developing some pictures I thought I had lost when the light began flashing. I didn't like the sound of the phone in the darkroom, so whenever the phone rang, a red light would flash. I pressed down on the speaker phone button, and said, "Hello."

"I said I would call you."

The sound of her sweet voice made me grin like an idiot. "You just didn't say when."

"Am I interrupting anything?"

"I'm in the darkroom," I reluctantly told her.

"You got me on that darn speakerphone."

"I have to keep my hands free when I'm developing pictures, you know that."

"I'll forgive you this time."

I felt a genuine sense of relief. I didn't want her to think that my work was more important than her. Many women thought they had to compete with my art, and truth be told, they did. But not Debrena Allen.

"I would like us to spend some quality time together," she said.

"What do you have in mind?"

"A face to face meeting."

"That sounds good. I like face to face."

"I know you do," she said, and I thought I detected a hint of sex in her voice.

I found myself getting aroused. Just the thought of her taking time out from her busy schedule did crazy things to my entire system. "When can we get together?"

CHAPTER 31

That is how I wound up at Stella's Diner, the place where I first met Debrena.

She wasn't there when I walked in, and I hadn't expected her to be. As a diva, Debrena had to make a grand entrance, and she never disappointed me. She came wearing oversized dark shades, a white cotton vee neck top, a frilly, feminine pink and yellow skirt, and open-toed sandals. She also carried a light tan, studded purse over her shoulder. She had some words with the owner of the establishment before finally coming over to me.

I was itching to snap a picture, but I left my camera at my loft, determined to give her my undivided attention. I stood when she came toward me and pulled out a chair for her. She gave me a bright smile before she sat down across from me. "Sit next to me," she said.

I found myself so close to her that I was inhaling her perfume and sharing her menu. Even though it was lunch time, we both ordered breakfast. I couldn't wait for the waitress to take our orders so that I could be alone with her. I said, "So how have you been?"

She looked at me strangely. "You mean since four days ago?"

I laughed, embarrassed like I had been caught stealing. "Four days seemed so long."

She looked at me strangely again, and I began to sweat. How

was I going to get this woman back into my bed when I couldn't even engage her in a decent conversation?

"What I meant was—"

"Relax, Choice," Debrena suggested.

Before I could take a deep breath and count to ten, Debrena said, "Were you satisfied with Lorrie's work on your project?"

"Lorrie was great. She really knows her stuff."

"Will you use her again?"

"Of course I will. Does she think I won't?"

"She thinks that you might have some hard feelings because she took your place in bed."

I paused because I felt the way I answered that particular question would determine my future with Debrena. "I have no hard feelings against Lorrie. What you and Lorrie have is just...different."

"Which means you don't think sex is just sex?"

"Sex is what it is," I began tentatively, then quickly added, "but there's different expressions of sex. The sex you have with Lorrie is a different expression."

"Did you feel that way when you saw the videotape of me in bed with another woman?"

"I was shocked. I was angry. Because of our relationship, I didn't want to share you with anyone."

"Things are not always what they seem, Choice. I won't deny it. That was me with the women on the tape. I won't even deny that she made me come. But I didn't know her, I don't know her, Janis drugged me and set me up."

Everything she said cut my heart to pieces like confetti.

"What you saw on that tape was me being raped. You know I'm not a drinker, but Janis got me to drink and put something in it. When she got me to her hotel room I thought I was having a sex dream. I couldn't look her in the face afterwards because I thought I had sex with her, and I knew I wasn't feeling Janis like that. At the time, I wasn't feeling *any* woman like that."

I nodded, trying hard to understand all that she was telling me. It made me hate Janis Wilson even more. But mixed up in my hate was pity for a woman who would drug another woman and put her in such a compromising sexual situation.

"Don't feel sorry for me, Choice," Debrena said because I didn't say anything.

"It's not that," I quickly replied. "It's just that I didn't know, and now I do. I hope I never jump to any quick judgments again."

"That's a great lesson to learn."

I suddenly saw Lorrie in another light, a better light. I saw her as someone who was helping Debrena heal herself. The waitress came back to our table with our meals.

As soon as the waitress left, Debrena said, "With all that out in the open, do you trust me, Choice?"

I nodded, my mouth filled with cheese omelet and home fries.

"Because I want you to do something," Debrena told me, turning in her chair to face me. "I want you to do a little something for me."

CHAPTER 32

"What did Debrena want you to do?" Curtis asked, but it was obvious that he was distracted by the big ass, banana yellow girl that walked pass our table in a black, skin tight cat suit. His eyes moved from her to another girl, not as provocatively dressed, but another good looker. He reminded me of a man watching a tennis match, his head moving from one end of the court to the other, trying to keep up with all the action.

We were at Malika's Place again. I didn't notice any damage from the fashion show riot. That wild scene was uncharacteristic of the class and sophistication I usually associated with Malika's Place.

The music playing was by Miles Davis. I had done some research on trumpet players last summer when I met Stan Allen, Debrena's father, a jazz trumpet player. The song was "In A Silent Way."

With the cool jazz music and the hot ladies, Curtis was in a bachelor's paradise. As Curtis brought his drink to his lips, I leaned forward so that I was right in his face. I watched him drink, and then said, "Debrena wants me to have sex with Lorrie."

Curtis looked at me bug eyed, and choked on his drink. "What?" he said staring at me, his eyes watering as he wiped his face with a red cocktail napkin.

I sat back with a self-satisfied smirk on my face. "You heard me."

"Brother Man…," Curtis began, and then couldn't seem to finish the thought. Then he leaned into me. "Are you serious?"

I allowed myself a soft chuckle. I loved having Curtis look at me in a different light. He always gave me the impression, because I didn't dress as slick as he did, that I was some kind of country nigga that just didn't have it together.

"You in bed with two hot honeys?"

"Not all of us in bed together."

"One at a time? That's still off the hook."

"Not one at a time."

"What? You watching the both of them together, and then jumping in?"

"No."

"Choice, what in the hell are you talking about then?"

"Debrena wants me to have sex with Lorrie while she watches."

Curtis fell back in his chair like I had sent a fist into his fore-head. Then he looked at me like he had never seen me before. "And where was all this discussed?"

"I was trying to tell you before you got distracted by that young lady in the cat suit; I had lunch yesterday with Debrena, at Stella's Diner."

Curtis shook his head. "Well, Brother Man, all I can say is, when is it going to go down?"

I stopped smiling. "That's the strange thing about it."

"What's strange about that? I know you're going to jump on that."

"Debrena said she would give me some time to think about it; to call her when I made up my mind."

Curtis became indignant. "What's to think about? You know you got to represent, Choice."

"It's not that simple."

"Man, if you can't handle it, I know a brother who can. Me."

"Listen to me, Curtis. We are not talking about some fantasy island stuff here. This is real sex with real people."

"That makes it even better. Jump on that. You got two freaky honeys that want to get their freak on, it's a once in a lifetime opportunity. If that was me, I would've signed up for the whole tour right then and there."

"It's not that simple," I said in a soft voice. "I want to get Debrena back, that's why I accepted her lunch invitation."

"So now you get two for the price of one. What's so hard about accepting that?"

"I don't want Lorrie, I want Debrena," I said, getting a little too loud. "Sex with two women is your fantasy, not mine."

After a few moments, Curtis said, "Brother Man, I'm trying so hard to understand you. I know you got to look before you leap, but I think you're taking this to a whole other level."

"I just can't figure out why Debrena wants me to do this."

"'Cause she's a freak," Curtis said, and then smiled broadly.

"I think it's more than that."

Curtis continued to shake his head. "Brother Man, what are you going to do?"

"I'm going to do what Debrena suggested. I'm going to think about it."

Curtis just shook his head, sipped his drink, and continued to watch the fine honeys as they walked by.

I suddenly regretted telling him anything.

CHAPTER 33

The next day I got together with my crew. We met in the same conference room at NTA where we met before the *Urban Vibe* shoot. I stood at the head of the long conference table with Princess and Lorrie sitting on my right side and Lyedecker and Karen sitting on my left.

"I'm not going to hold you long," I promised. "I just wanted to let you know how much I appreciated all of your hard work. I spoke with Carrie this morning and she told me that the client is more than pleased. You all deserve a round of applause."

I began the clapping, and then they joined in.

Afterwards, Lyedecker asked, "When are we going to do it again?"

He kept on touching his neck as if the tie he wore was choking him. "Soon," I answered. "Soon for all of you. I will be in touch."

The young intern looked at me impatiently.

"In the meantime, enjoy your success," I said, "and very soon I will show you the photos from the shoot. I spent all of last night developing the film and producing a contact sheet for the client. When the art director at *Urban Vibe* decides what shots they want to use I'll blow the photos up and invite you to the loft to check them out."

Everyone murmured their approval.

"One last thing," I said.

On the table in front of me was a black leather folder. Lyedecker clapped when I opened it up and he saw the white envelopes inside.

"Now that's what I'm talking about," the young intern said as I lifted the envelopes. I believed in paying my crew as soon as possible. I handed the NTA checks out and they all thanked me before they left.

"I didn't expect this so soon," Lorrie said as she took the check I held out to her. "Thanks for the opportunity."

I thought she was going to say something else, so I waited.

"Well…," she began. "Thanks again, Choice."

Before she could turn away, I said softly, "We need to talk."

Lorrie nodded.

CHAPTER 34

It wasn't a fancy restaurant like Malika's Place. And it wasn't even in Elizabeth. As a matter of fact, it was a restaurant in Cranford, New Jersey. But it offered a menu similar to Stella's Diner and it was far enough out of the way that we could eat and talk without running into anybody we knew. It was called The Rustic Mill, a nice quiet place with plenty of sunlight coming in through big picture windows.

"Thanks for joining me for lunch," I told Lorrie as we settled into our seats.

"I'm not that hungry," Lorrie told me for the second time that afternoon.

"I know, but we need to talk."

"Because of what Debrena wants us to do."

I nodded.

"I can't stay long," Lorrie told me, and I nodded again. "I told my mother that I'd be back after a short meeting at NTA."

"I understand. We could've talked in the conference room, but this is better. No interruptions."

"What do you want to say?"

"Let's order first," I suggested. "That way there will be fewer interruptions."

Lorrie nodded, and I signaled for a waitress. We ordered salas drinks, cranberry juice for me, and a peach Snapple for her. She looked at me like we were chess players and she expected me to make the first move.

"How do you feel about this?" I asked.

Lorrie laughed softly. "You don't beat around the bush."

"I don't want to waste your time. Are you down with this?"

"This is something that D wants. I love her, I want to see her happy."

"So you're doing this for Debrena."

"Isn't that why you're doing it?"

She had me there; I didn't know her well enough to have any real desire for her.

"It has to be safe sex," Lorrie told me, and I sensed some anxiety on her part.

"I'll bring condoms. Are you comfortable with this?"

"What are you worried about, Choice? That I'll lay there like a dead fish? That you won't find me attractive when I'm naked in front of you? That you won't be able to get it up?"

"Believe it or not, I'm thinking about you. How will you feel when it's over? Will you feel used? Will you hate me? Hate Debrena?"

"You're making this a little too serious. It's not that deep. I know what I'm getting into. I'm a consenting adult."

The waitress returned with our food.

Before the waitress left, Lorrie said, "Excuse me, I need to make a quick call."

I watched as Lorrie walked to the front of the restaurant. I thanked the waitress. Because my appetite was nonexistent, I found myself looking out of the window. I saw Lorrie, on the sidewalk, on her cell phone. Her face was tight as if she was engaged in a tense conversation. I found myself raising my camera. There was intensity in her face, but also tenderness. Then she laughed, and I saw her as an alluring and sexy young woman, like she was at the airport with Debrena. I snapped her picture, and right then and there I felt I wanted to know her, and not just between the sheets. When she came back into the restaurant I was still moving my salad around on my plate, mixing it with the blue cheese still moving my salad around on my plate, mixing it with the blue cheese dressing.

"Could I get a doggy bag? I'd hate to waste your money."

"Do you have a dog?" I asked, and Lorrie laughed.

"No."

We laughed together.

"I had to call my mother. She had a stroke a couple of years ago. She's doing all right, but she's on some new medication. I called to make sure she took her medicine with some food in her stomach."

I felt that she had just shared something with me.

"I'll call Debrena," I told Lorrie.

"Okay." Because she had followed me in her car there was no reason for her to wait. She got a waitress to wrap her food and walked out of the restaurant. I saw her get into her car and drive off.

As for Debrena, I thought the best thing for me to do was to tell her what she wanted to hear.

CHAPTER 35

I found myself alone in my darkroom. Several days had passed since I met with Lorrie and I still hadn't called Debrena. I was having second thoughts. Whenever I found the courage to call Debrena I would step away from the phone and find something else to do.

Every time I ran into Curtis he was my biggest cheerleader. "Get in the game, Brother Man. You got to be in it to win it."

What do you have to lose? I asked myself, trying to think like Curtis and all the other men who could only dream about being in my situation.

Am I a fool? Was I afraid? Was there some performance anxiety on my part?

I never had a problem getting and maintaining an erection. Still, I didn't see myself as an exhibitionist.

Was I just a pawn in some sick game that Debrena was playing?

It had been a year since I made love to Debrena. I always playfully called her a freak, but maybe since we had parted she had become that and more. Perhaps all she wanted me to do was become a vehicle to take her freakiness to another level.

What it came down to was not what Debrena wanted. Not what Lorrie wanted. Or what Curtis thought I should do. It came down to what I wanted, and how I would feel after it went down. If I didn't call Debrena I got the distinct impression that I would never hear from her again. She had given me a way to get back into her life, and if I didn't pick up on it, then it was shame on me.

Every morning I worked out like I was preparing for a championship fight. I wanted to look good in the bedroom with Lorrie, especially with Debrena watching. *Would my sexy moves with Lorrie make Debrena realize what a mistake it was for her to drop me as her lover?*

I thought about how my body would look to Lorrie. *Would she find me a turn on?*

Or would I be a joke?

I recalled the "Not joke."

After a man wined and dined a woman and got her into his bed, he asked her. "How was I, baby? Did I satisfy ya?"

Pulling on her clothes, the woman said, "It was okay. There were too many 'nots' in it."

"Knots?" the man asked.

"It was *not* long enough, *not* hard enough, and *not* big enough!"

What brought me to my decision more than anything else were shots I took of Debrena and Lorrie standing outside of NTA and in Newark International Airport. The two of them together was truly fascinating, in their diva mode, pulling the attention from almost everyone in the airport. What caught my shooter's eye was the love and quiet affection between them that was intense, but not vulgar.

I imagined them at home admiring each other, caressing each other, bringing each other to a climax, and sharing none of that with a man. Perhaps feeling that no man was worthy of seeing that kind of interaction between them. Although I was fully aware that I would be having sex with only Lorrie, I knew Debrena would be there and her presence would add to the sensuality of the encounter. In a way I would be having sex with them both.

I went on to develop the shots I had taken of Lorrie outside The Rustic Mill. I didn't realize how many shots I had taken until I hung them up around me in the darkroom. The concern and

compassion that Lorrie showed in those shots made her even sex-
ier to me, like our coupling would be something truly special and
emotional, and not just some side show for Debrena's benefit.

I knew Debrena from our hot summer together, and I knew
the heat she could generate when she was turned on. When she
stopped thinking self-consciously and really let herself go, when
she got so caught up that she didn't care what her hair looked like
or how much she sweated, or how much she stank, or if she farted.
During those times we had our most intense sexual encounters.
We would go at it so hard and heavy that we would fall asleep
immediately afterwards. We would totally exhaust our bodies and
our minds and souls. All we had and all we needed was each
other.

The memory of that completeness made me want Debrena
even more.

Lorrie was a way for me to get back to the special heat I had
not experienced with anyone before or after Debrena. So I called
her. The phone rang three times and I panicked because I thought
I'd have to talk to her answering machine.

"Yes," Debrena answered, sounding like we had been talking
for hours and were now continuing our conversation after a short
break.

"This is Choice."

"Yes, Choice."

"Did Lorrie tell you we had lunch together?"

"Yes, she told me."

"I don't want to hurt Lorrie. You know, embarrass her in any
way."

"Choice, Lorrie is a big girl."

"Let's do this."

"The way I want it?"

"Is there any other way?"

"Not this time."

"You'll set everything up?"

"Yes."

"I'll be there."

I hung up the phone without saying goodbye.

CHAPTER 36

That night I spent almost an hour in the bathroom, showering, scrubbing and rinsing, clipping my finger and toe nails. I rubbed lotion over my body, then got dressed in my white double breasted jacket with a black muscle shirt and black pants. I slipped my bare feet into a pair of black loafers. The last thing I did before I left my loft was put a three pack of Trojans in the inside pocket of my jacket.

As I sat in my ride, just as I was about to get out, a song that I hadn't heard in a long time came on and froze me behind the wheel; it was "At Midnight (My Love Will Lift You Up)" as recorded by the super band Rufus, with Chaka Khan on lead vocals. This song could be the soundtrack for what was about to happen between me, Lorrie, and Debrena. It's funny how songs have a way of setting the stage that way.

It was just twenty minutes before midnight when I got out of my ride and walked up the cobble-stoned pathway to Debrena's house. Before I could knock, Debrena opened the door. She wore a black leotard top and a short denim skirt. Her feet were bare. She smiled as if to say, *glad you made it*. Perhaps she thought that I would cop out at the last minute. I had some anxiety, but the adrenalin that pumped through my body made me more than ready for what was about to go down.

"I meant to tell you," Debrena began as I walked pass her and into the house. "I really like the way your hair turned out."

I nodded, touching the hair that I had let loose that night; there was no leather string to tie it into a ponytail.

I was somewhat surprised to see no one in the living room.

"Lorrie is here," Debrena assured me.

I didn't say anything as I sat on the sofa. I hadn't been inside Debrena's house in a year. So many memories rushed into my mind and flooded my senses.

Toni Braxton's soothing voice filled the room.

I wanted to ask where Lorrie was as Debrena sat in the black leather chair opposite the sofa. Instead, I took off my jacket and draped it over the back of the sofa. That was when Lorrie came into the living room. She wore a yellow body suit with a long black skirt that had deep splits up both sides. Like Debrena, she was barefoot. She looked over at me, then said, "Good evening, Choice."

"Good evening, Lorrie," I replied, sounding a lot more formal than I intended to.

Debrena chuckled, obviously amused by our awkwardness. "Now that we know each other, maybe we should get the show on the road."

Looking straight at me, Lorrie said, "Would you like something to drink?"

"No, nothing," I said, looking straight at Debrena, letting her know that I was not amused about her taking this situation lightly.

"I'm going to have something," Lorrie announced. "I have some wine in the kitchen."

She left and Debrena turned toward me. "A little nervous, perhaps?"

"Are you sure you know what you're doing?" I asked, leaning forward and whispering so that Lorrie wouldn't hear us.

"This is going to be the best night of your life," Debrena assured me, but she didn't look happy.

"We'll see about that."

Lorrie returned holding two glasses of wine. She sat one in front of me on a coffee table. "Just in case you change your mind," she said, and then sipped from her glass.

Standing near me, I observed how solidly built Lorrie was. There didn't seem to be an ounce of fat on her body. She stood and drank her wine and swayed to the music, her eyes closed. She didn't open them until her glass was empty. "Dance with me," Lorrie said when Toni Braxton's "I Love Me Some Him" came on. I stood and Lorrie set her glass on the coffee table. When she straightened up I was so close to her that her hard nipples brushed my chest. I pushed into her as we moved slowly to the music.

There was no hint of a bra. Her sweet perfume filled my nostrils and made my head light. I began to sweat. With Lorrie's head on my chest, I looked over her shoulder to see Debrena looking intently at us.

When an up-tempo song came on I continued to slow drag with Lorrie. Her body was solid and warm against mine.

"Kiss her," Debrena suggested from her seat.

I got a little offended because I didn't want to be directed by Debrena. I wanted things to unfold naturally and I wanted some control over what was going on.

Lorrie stepped back, and turned her face up to me. I ran my hands up the sides of her slim hips, and felt no hint of a panty line. It made me eager to pull her into me as I bent my head to claim her mouth. First it was just her lips on my lips, and then suddenly her mouth opened and I found myself in her warm wetness, searching her wine flavored mouth as I ran my hands up and down her hips. Because there was no resistance on her part, I began to explore her body, letting my hands roam her waist and then move to her back. I even hesitantly palmed her ass to push her further into me.

"Don't hold back, Choice," Debrena coached from the side-lines.

The more Debrena talked, the more Lorrie melted into me, like she was trying to push her way through my body. I wanted to ask Lorrie, *Are you okay with this?* But we both had come too far to entertain that question.

"Come on, Choice," Debrena coaxed, "make love to that woman."

Love had nothing to do with it. With Lorrie pressed up tight against me, and searching for my mouth, it was all about ego. My big, fat male ego.

And Debrena wanted a show.

Lorrie gasped as I suddenly grabbed her shoulders and spun her around. This way she had her back to me and was facing Debrena. That was when I pulled down the top of Lorrie's yellow body suit, leaving her torso bare. I pressed my crotch into her round ass as I brought my hands up in front of her, making her grunt and moan as I massaged her full, firm bare breasts. I ran my lips up and down her neck, making her moan even more as I put my hands into the splits at the side of her long black skirt. I touched hot flesh as I looked over Lorrie's shoulder at Debrena.

"Wild man, wild man," Debrena whispered as I completely took over Lorrie's body.

Lorrie turned her head toward me and I claimed her mouth again, my tongue was a spear that separated her lips and plunged into the deepest part of her mouth. Her ass pressed against my hard-on and I felt that the only thing for me to do was to bend her over and take her from behind.

"I think you two need a bedroom."

Lorrie stumbled away from me like she was drunk.

I looked over at Debrena, expecting to see a self-satisfied smirk on her face. What I saw was more like fear, like she had set something in motion that she couldn't control. Debrena lowered her eyes and walked out of the room, following behind Lorrie.

With them both gone, I stood in the living room by myself. I looked at the wooden framed clock hanging on the wall, just seconds before midnight. No turning back now. I walked down the hallway leading to Debrena's bedroom, pulled my shirt out of my pants and kicked off my shoes. As I walked into the bedroom, I stripped off my shirt and let my pants fall to the floor.

You want a show? My mind screamed. *I'll give you a show.*

CHAPTER 37

When I finally got home I didn't make it pass the living room. I threw my jacket across the room and it fell about a foot away from the couch. I kicked off my shoes and unbuckled my pants. On the drive home from Debrena's all I could think about was a nice hot shower but the couch was too inviting.

I stripped down to my boxers and lay on the couch. I found myself staring up at the ceiling, but this time I wasn't in Debrena's bed. What happened there was amazing. It took sex to another level, at least for me. I thought I had prepared myself for a wild night, but I could not have prepared myself for what actually went down.

They were both in the bedroom with Debrena standing between the full length mirror and the bed where Lorrie laid sprawled out nude. Seeing all of Lorrie like that stunned me. Somehow I thought we would take it slow and just ease into the situation. Obviously that was not the way it was going to be. My eyes traveled up Lorrie's long bare legs to the slightly parted thighs that revealed her shaved crotch. The thick folds of her womanhood were dark and glistening wet. I also couldn't help but notice her prominent nipples, dark brown against her honey colored skin.

"Are you ready?" Debrena called out to me, pulling me away from staring at Lorrie.

I nodded, but didn't feel totally confident. *Was I ready?* I really couldn't say if I was. But I did know that this was my time. And Lorrie's time. When I found my voice, I said, "I'll be right back."

I almost tripped over my pants and shirt as I stepped back out into the hallway. I kicked my clothes away from me like they were entangling vines I had to rid myself of. I walked down the hall still wearing my Tommy Hilfiger boxer shorts. I walked into the living room and over to my discarded double-breasted jacket. From the inside pocket I pulled out my package of condoms.

I tried real hard not to think about what I was doing as I walked back to the bedroom.

This time when I stood in the doorway, Debrena was on the bed with Lorrie. They were whispering when I came into the room and continued for a few seconds until Lorrie noticed me and gently tapped Debrena's shoulder. Debrena glanced at me and then whispered something to Lorrie.

I couldn't hear what she said, but Lorrie reacted to it by nodding her head solemnly.

That was when Debrena kissed Lorrie. Debrena's tongue went out and parted Lorrie's lips. Lorrie moaned as she pressed her face into Debrena's. For a moment it was like I wasn't standing there, like they were all alone. As they kissed, Debrena took her hands from Lorrie's face and let them run along Lorrie's long, nude body. She didn't pull away until she had run her hands all over Lorrie's thighs and down into the valley of her womanhood.

My hard-on pushed at the front of my Tommy Hilfiger shorts. *There was definitely no turning back now.*

Lorrie moaned softly, then Debrena removed her hand and got up from the bed. Debrena looked at me with eyes glazed with lust. I expected her to say something like "It's all yours" or "Do your thing," but that wasn't the case. Debrena said nothing as she walked toward the space between the full-length mirror and the bed.

I stepped toward the bed.

Terry B.

I sighed deeply as I looked up at the ceiling in my loft. I sat up and shook my head, as if that would clear all the confusion. It was like there were too many cobwebs in the dusky attic of my brain. I knew I wouldn't see Lorrie again unless I called her for a job. As for Debrena, I didn't know when I would see her again or how I could approach her. I had spent an hour at her home, in her bedroom, because she had invited me. *Should I take that as an open invitation to invite myself back? Did I live up to all of her expectations? Did I put on the show that she wanted to see?*

CHAPTER 38

The Sunday Jazz Brunch at Malika's Place combined good food with live entertainment. As I sat with Curtis, a four man group played the music of Miles Davis. Curtis leaned forward with his elbows on the table, one ear toward me and one ear toward the music; his hands folded together and leaning on his chin. "She was naked like that?" Curtis whispered.

"Spread out without a stitch on."

"You just jumped right on in."

"Not yet."

"Man, I would've just jumped in."

"And you would've been that Two Minute Man."

Curtis chuckled softly. "Not me, Brother Man. I know how to exercise self control. I know how to pace myself."

"Yeah, right. Well, her legs were wide open and she looked directly at me. I could see that she was real wet down there."

"Lorrie couldn't wait to get the bone?"

"I don't know about that. I didn't think she needed a whole lot of foreplay, but I couldn't see myself just plunging into her."

"So you had to pat the kitty kat."

"You could say that. I rubbed between her thighs, and she was soft and damp down there. She opened her legs even more as I moved up to kiss her."

"Man, you a regular Black Casanova."

"Whatever," I said smiling. "Anyway, I kissed her and she ran her hands up and down my bare back. Her mouth was as sweet as honey. And then she moved her hands to the front of my boxers."

"I told you, she couldn't wait to get some of that." Curtis began to get louder than necessary.

"Lorrie grabbed me with both hands and I almost lost it. I had to bite down on my lip and think about Chinese arithmetic to keep from coming. I figured she would just lay back and let me do my thing. I had no idea that she would be that aggressive."

"I hate when a honey lays there like a dead fish. Like she's doing a brother a favor. If she can't move her ass I don't want her. I'm not asking her to be a porn star princess like Heather Hunter, but she better do more than just lay there. You know what I'm saying?"

I nodded in agreement.

"So then what?"

"I kissed her on the mouth, and then moved down her body, running my tongue over her breasts. They were round and full with dark brown nipples." I felt I was giving too many details, but I wanted to give Curtis so much that he would think that I had no more to tell.

"Man, do the damn thing," Curtis hissed as if he were coaching me from the sidelines.

"You know I had to wrap it up. When I put the condom on, Lorrie's eyes were still on me. She didn't close her eyes until I began moving inside her. She was tight, but wet so I kept on pushing into her deeper and deeper. I was really surprised by the tightness."

"She probably hadn't had it in a long time. Man, I can't understand that as fine as she is. She's probably one of those honeys that gots to be in love to give it up."

"I don't think she was in love with me that night."

"Don't get all quiet on me now."

"She…um…moaned loudly as I got deep inside her."

"Knocked the bottom out of it, didn't you?"

"I don't know about that, but she wrapped her legs around

me. And she came, exploding like a volcano under me."

"Did you bust a nut?"

"Yeah. When she came she held onto my legs and arms and I continued to push in and out of her. I realized that she wasn't going to let me go until I came. I reached beneath her and grabbed her hot, soft ass and ran in and out of her until I closed my eyes and let myself go."

"My man," Curtis said, sounding like a proud father. "You took care of business big time."

I couldn't help but feel good. Even though there were many things that disturbed me about that night, I could say that I rose to the challenge.

"And Debrena was there the whole time just watching," Curtis remarked, shaking his head, envy and amazement on his face. "I didn't know you had it like that, Brother Man."

I sat back basking in the glow of Curtis's compliment.

"You know I got to run, to see a client."

"On a Sunday?"

"It isn't the best time, but you got to strike while the iron is hot. If I get this it will mean work for you too."

"What do you have in the works?"

Curtis smiled as he signaled for a waitress. "Big things, Brother Man. But I don't want to go into it right now. When it's a done deal I'll bring you in."

Curtis continued. "Besides, you don't want to jump into a heavy work schedule right now anyway."

"Why not?"

"You have to recuperate from that heavy sex scene that Debrena roped you into."

"I'm okay."

"Ready to go again?"

"I got the impression that was a one time only scene."

The waitress came over to our table and Curtis paid for our meal with a credit card. When she left, Curtis said, "I'm sure you can worm your way back into that. Your girl Debrena looks like a real freak."

"You saw Debrena?" I asked, surprised.

Curtis looked at me like a man who had said too much. "When did you see Debrena?" I pressed.

Curtis spoke like a man who had just come out of a coma. "Today's Sunday, it had to be Friday. Right here as a matter of fact. I was talking to the owners, trying to set up a showcase for some new talent. Your girl came to speak to Malika, but I didn't say too much to her."

I was surprised that he had said anything to her at all.

"Don't look so worried," Curtis said, trying to read the puzzlement on my face. "I didn't say anything about the freaky scene you had planned with her and Lorrie."

"Did you tell her that you knew me?"

"I think I told her that I saw her picture in your loft. Then I told her that she looked better in person. You know, trying to soup her up a little bit. But she didn't stay long, she had finished her business with Malika and left."

The waitress brought back the black leather billfold with Curtis's credit card and receipt. "You can leave a tip," Curtis told me and stood as I reached into my back pocket for my wallet. "I got to run."

Then Curtis was gone.

CHAPTER 39

L ater that evening I tried to do some work, but couldn't concentrate. I realized I needed some supplies which gave me a legitimate reason to stop.

Get some supplies and come back to work, I told myself as I grabbed my car keys.

Inside my ride, I pushed in a CD that I'd once used for a shoot. On the CD were Donny Hathaway, Smokey Robinson, Rick James, James Brown, and Al Green. It was a nice mix and I usually enjoyed it, but this night I was too distracted, thinking about my night in Debrena's bed with Lorrie.

After I had come, I made sure that I didn't press my weight onto Lorrie. I fell off to the side and rested beside her as I looked up at the ceiling. Lorrie lay beside me also looking up at the ceiling, her arm thrown across my heaving and sweaty chest. When I opened my eyes I noticed some movement at the side of the bed. It was Debrena.

On my way to the photographic supply store I found myself driving through Debrena's neighborhood and double parking on the narrow street where she lived. I parked just a few houses down from hers, close enough to see who went in or out of her house, but far enough not to be seen.

The street was quiet on this early Sunday evening and the

supplies I needed could be bought at the local CVS so I was in no big hurry.

I couldn't see myself walking up to Debrena's door and knocking. *Was I supposed to wait for her call?*

Suddenly, the front door to Debrena's house opened and Lorrie stepped out. She quickly walked down the walkway that led to the street.

Right then and there I knew it was time for me to back out of there.

That was when Debrena came out of the house. She shouted something at Lorrie, but I was too far away to hear. Lorrie looked irritated as she continued to walk toward the street. Debrena reached out and grabbed her arm. They stood facing each other, while Debrena talked and Lorrie held her body stiffly. Lorrie shook her head as Debrena pointed her finger at her face.

I slowly backed my ride down the street.

There was the sound of a loud car horn from behind.

In the rear-view-mirror I saw that I had almost run into a car coming up behind me. I stopped abruptly and put my blinkers on so that the car could go around.

When I looked ahead, I saw Lorrie's car moving down the street and Debrena walking back to her house.

Much to my relief, I hadn't been spotted.

What was happening to me? Was I becoming some obsessed fool?

CHAPTER 40

I didn't make it to CVS. I was too shaken by the situation I had put myself in. Once at the intersection, I made my turn and rode back to my loft and the sanctuary of my darkroom.

I was able to develop some prints from the shots I had taken at the fashion show at Malika's Place. I developed the majority of them, but the ones I studied most carefully were the shots of Debrena.

In her bedroom that night, Debrena had gotten more involved than I expected. I guess watching me and Lorrie having sex fired her libido. When I opened my eyes and saw her standing near the bed, I was startled.

"You can do it again," Debrena said.

I worked hard in the darkroom as if my exertions would erase the kaleidoscope of images that haunted me.

Before I could sit completely up, Debrena pressed a hand into my chest. She threw her bare leg over my thigh, rubbing her damp womanhood along the thick column of my leg. I looked up at her, hoping that she wasn't going to tease me.

I became rock hard when Debrena bent her head and parted my lips with her long, wet tongue. She got between my thighs, stretching out on the bed, her perfect round ass sticking up, and grabbed my manhood. As I got harder and longer, she took me in her mouth. I wiggled shamelessly on the bed as Debrena made magic with her mouth, she even put that Deep Throat action on me and I almost came. It was exquisite torture and I never wanted her to stop. I felt some movement on the bed next to me, but because my eyes were shut I couldn't tell what was going on.

I opened my eyes in time to see Debrena reach for a condom, open it up, put it in her mouth and then rolled it down my hard-on. With her delicate fingers, she smoothed the protection over me, covering me to the hilt, her hands hot even through the latex. I grunted loudly when Debrena used both of her hands to open herself to fit her slick, tight, hairless womanhood over my hard-on, then slammed her slick, wet bottom down on me.

My head fell back as Debrena rode me. I shut my eyes and stroked her breasts and played with her nipples. Then I lowered my hand to squeeze a cheek of her ass. Debrena whispered in my ear: "Do it, baby. Do that shit."

Then her bouncing became even more intense and she cried out, losing control, trembling as she came. Her wild movements and the complete abandonment she displayed pushed me over the edge, and I came, raising my knees as my orgasm hit me like a punch in the stomach. My balls ached as I released myself. I felt like I had emptied everything I had inside me as Debrena collapsed upon my sweat soaked, heaving chest.

When I finally opened my eyes I realized Lorrie had left the room.

I pulled the cord in the darkroom and plunged the room into total darkness.

I stumbled out of the darkroom like a man being chased by demons.

In the living room, I sat on the couch and grabbed my phone. I speed dialed the number and connected with L.A.

"Londa," I said into the phone as soon as it stopped ringing. "I need to talk to you."

"Who is this?" a man's voice asked me.

I tripped out. "I'm trying to get in touch with Londa Newberry."

"Who should I say is calling?"

I disconnected the call. Londa was a young, single woman and just because we had sex once doesn't mean we were together. So why was I upset that a man answered her phone?

The phone rang and rang until I could no longer ignore it.

"Yes," I said harshly, thinking it was Londa.

"Choice?" It was Lorrie.

CHAPTER 41

L orrie wanted to meet. My instinct was to say no and hang up the phone, but I needed to know what Lorrie had to say. I suggested Rahway River Park, not too far from Elizabeth. I drove to the park and got out of my ride when Lorrie pulled up in her dark blue Toyota Camry. We sat in the front seat of her car with the windows down.

"D wasn't supposed to participate," Lorrie said, looking straight ahead, her hands tight around the steering wheel of her parked car. "She was just supposed to watch us. No offense to you, Choice, but D jumping in like that blew my mind. I never imagined it going down like that."

"You're telling me that you and Debrena never did anything like that before?"

"Never, Choice. That's why I had to leave the room."

"I thought all that was part of Debrena's plan."

"She never told me anything about it. After I spoke to her, she told me that she just got caught up in the moment."

I became angry. It sounded like Debrena, not caring about anyone, but herself. I also felt a little sorry for Lorrie.

"How did this whole thing get started? Were you and Debrena sitting around scheming on me?"

"It's a lot deeper than that, Choice. It wasn't all about you. D was putting me to the test."

She told me about her two friends, Marcy Chase and Angela King, and how Marcy took a dare that proved her love for Angela.

"Even though I did exactly what D asked," Lorrie continued. "D seems more insecure than ever."

"You two need to stop playing games," I told Lorrie, sounding a lot more self-righteous than I intended.

"It wasn't a game for me, Choice," Lorrie said sadly. "I love D, and I want us to be together forever."

"You slept with me and find out that Debrena is still not ready to commit. I would think that you'd be a little hurt."

"I'm not hurt. Maybe a little disappointed because I thought that this would bring us closer together. Now D feels guilty about what she asked me to do. She looks at me and sees how miserable and confused I am and she feels uncomfortable around me now. I've tried to let her know I got into that bed with my eyes wide open. I was a consenting adult even though I never had sex with a man."

I looked hard at Lorrie. I had assumed she was bi-sexual like Debrena. "You gave up your virginity for Debrena?"

Lorrie looked at me with sad eyes. "I gave up more than that, Choice. I have always identified myself as a lesbian. I never wanted to get into the label game. You know, speculating who's lesbian, bi-sexual, tri-sexual, bi-curious. But thanks to you and D, I'm all caught up in that confusion. I can't say what I am now; I responded to you, big time, I had an orgasm with you."

"Have you told Debrena all that you told me?"

"I've tried, but she gets so defensive when we talk about that night. What I did with you was a lot more than walking around the block in my underwear. I just want D to acknowledge that, recognize that. That night changed me so much. I'm a new person now. I don't know who this new person is. And I can't blame it all on D. Or you."

CHAPTER 42

Lorrie

I stopped by D's house whenever she was away on a business trip. I would collect her mail and put it inside on the table in the foyer. This way the mail wouldn't pile up, and any potential intruder would get the impression that someone was home.

I always rang the bell before I used the key she had given me. Even during the day it was a little scary for me going into an empty house. I lived with my mother and was used to having someone to come home to, unlike D. Sometimes I felt a little sorry for her.

It was a Friday, days after my meeting with Choice. As I made my way onto D's porch, to my surprise, there was no mail in the box. I figured it was a day when the mailman had nothing for the Allen residence. When I opened the front door, I found D standing in the living room, dressed in a red China silk robe.

"I saw you coming up the walk."

The robe clung to her from top to mid-thigh, making her long, well shaped dancer's legs look even longer. "I didn't expect you to be back so soon."

D had been in L.A. with Shai, Immature, IV Example, and Monteco, all MCA acts, doing their onstage choreography for a series of concerts at the Universal City Walk sponsored by L.A. Gear.

Ordinarily I would have hugged and kissed D, welcoming her back with open arms and legs. But the last time we spoke we both said some very nasty things, and because I stormed out of her house, there hadn't been any time to make up. Still, my body reacted to the closeness of her: I wanted to reach out and touch her.

"I was just running a bath," D told me, and then smiled shyly.

I followed her as she walked down the hall to the bathroom. By force of habit, I kicked off my sandals.

"I know you want to talk," D began.

"Don't you?"

D nodded. "I got something for you," D told me as she stopped in the hallway, and then walked over to a Neimann Marcus shopping bag and pulled something out. She handed me a Chanel wallet. "It's the hottest wallet this season."

I reluctantly took the wallet.

"I was a little uptight before I left. Partly because of the L.A Gear/MCA thing; but I got through that pretty good. At least everybody seemed all right with what I did. Sometimes they change things behind your back, but I've learned not to get all stressed over that. Come with me into the bathroom, so we can talk."

D reached for my hand, but I pulled away. "No sex until we get some things straight."

D smiled. "No sex?"

"Nothing until you show me some respect."

"What makes you think I don't respect you?"

"The way you spoke to me before you left."

"I told you that I had a lot on my mind," D said so defensively that I seriously thought about marching right out of her house.

"I am not going to let you treat me like shit, D. It's just not going to happen. If I let you do that I just wouldn't be able to respect myself. I'm not going to let you or anybody do that to me."

"I understand. I'm sorry if I said anything to make you feel less than a woman. I was loud and wrong, but like I said—"

"You had a lot on your mind."

"I figured you would understand."

"I could've if you would've broken it down for me, instead of covering it with your bullshit."

"My bullshit?"

"Yes, your bullshit. Be straight with me, D. I've always been straight with you. If you don't want to continue this relationship, I'll try real hard to understand that."

"Lorrie, why do you think I want to break up with you every time we have a little disagreement?"

"Because I know that—"

D held up a hand. "I have to check on my bath water."

"Okay," I said as she rushed down the hall.

CHAPTER 43

She sat on the edge of the tub, her hands testing the temperature of her bath water.

"It's still a little too hot," D said. "You were saying before I cut you off?"

"I think that sometimes you're afraid of what we have. What we mean to each other."

"Why would I be afraid of our love?"

"Maybe you're afraid it won't last. Maybe you think this is something temporary, like your relationship with that White girl."

D laughed, amused that I refused to call Tyra Woodstock by her name.

"We've been real tight since last summer, Lorrie. That means a lot to me."

"But sometimes I get the feeling that you don't think that we're going to last, like this whole thing will fall apart."

"I never said that," D snapped. "I've never been with anybody as long as I've been with you, Lorrie. It's been from one summer to the next, real tight."

I nodded.

"That means a lot to me," D said as she stood up beside the tub.

"It means a lot to me, too." She dropped her robe and stood naked before me.

"You want to join me?"

"I need to talk first." It was hard to resist her, her deep chocolate brown skin so silky smooth. But I had to let her know what was in my heart.

D stepped into the tub, laid down and pulled the sudsy water over her body like a warm blanket.

"You have to admit when you're wrong, D."

"What did I do that was so wrong?" She used her bath sponge over her shoulders and the top of her breasts.

"You make too light of my sacrifice."

D sighed heavily. "Your sacrifice?"

"What you asked me to do. With Choice."

"Lorrie, you have to admit Choice is a good looking brother."

"I don't care about that nonsense. I fucked Choice for you! That was my sacrifice!"

I began to cry.

D stepped out of the tub, dripping water everywhere and covered herself with her robe. She then pulled me from the doorway to comfort me and sat me down on the commode. She took the Chanel wallet from between my hands and placed it on the hamper. Because I had held my emotions in check for so long I found it so hard to stop crying.

"It's okay, baby." D whispered as she knelt beside me. "Let it all out."

"I'll get sick crying like this," I told her as she grabbed my hand. "What I did, it wasn't something trivial."

"I know that, baby. I would never make light of that. It was my crazy idea." "But I did want you to test me," I said, wiping my face and taking deep breaths. "But you hurt me bad, D. You hurt me so bad. Why did you have to join in?"

"What was I supposed to do?" She stood up and moved away from me. "Play with myself while you got down with Choice?"

"You know what you were supposed to do!" I shouted, pointing my finger up at her. "You made it a whole new thing!"

"Well excuse me for being a horny bitch!"

"It's more than that. It's like you can't stand to be left out of anything."

"They say the more the merrier," D said, her arms folded beneath her heaving breasts.

"Not when it comes to that. Not when I put myself out there like that. You turned my sacrifice into a freak show."

"For someone who claims she doesn't like men, you looked like you were enjoying yourself."

"But I wouldn't have been in that position if it wasn't for you. I wasn't trying to please him, or even myself; I did all that to please you. Can't you get that through your selfish head?"

After a few moments of silence, D said, "Lorrie, I'm sorry. I appreciated what you did for me. I shouldn't have asked you to do that."

"I wanted you to ask me. I wanted you to put me to the test."

"And you came through like a champ, Lorrie. I'll never, *ever,* ask you to do anything like that again. I love you and I am truly, *truly,* sorry. Please forgive me?"

I stood and pulled her into my arms. She kissed my neck and ran her hands up and down my body, making my clothes disappear beneath her hot hands. It wasn't long before I was naked. After more kissing and hugging, D removed her robe and I followed her out of the bathroom.

CHAPTER 44

Choice

I felt Lorrie's pain as she spoke in the park. After what seemed like twenty minutes of awkward silence, we went our separate ways.

Lorrie's burden left me drained. Why was I so easily sucked into Debrena's sick game? Did I really think that having sex with Lorrie would get me back with Debrena? If I hadn't thought that, why did I do it? Why did I take something from Lorrie that she had never given to any man?

If I hadn't had a meeting with Dany at NTA that day I would've never left the loft. I dragged myself out of bed and went through the motions of my Dirty Dozen, the series of exercises I always did to start my day. I felt defeated, like I had entered into a contest handicapped and came out the loser that I knew I would be.

When I walked into the conference room at the Nelson Talent Agency, I found Curtis sitting with Dany and Carrie. I couldn't remember the last time the four of us had sat down for a meeting together.

"Good morning, Choice," Dany said as I sat next to Curtis in the middle of the long boardroom table.

Carrie waved at me from her place at the head of the table and

Curtis slapped me gently on the back.

"What's going on?" I asked.

"I know you thought you were just meeting with my daughter," Carrie said, "but something major has come up that I felt we all needed to be aware of."

"Is this about the project you mentioned on the phone?" I asked.

"Correct," Carrie assured me. "It's the *Latina Woman* fashion magazine. It's a great project and I'm very glad that NTA was selected for it."

Dany nodded.

Curtis sat nonchalant and debonair beside her, his body language saying he was the man for the job.

"I'm still doing the photos?"

"Of course," Carrie assured me. "In my mind, there's no one better. But it seems we have competition," Carrie stated and I sat up in my chair. "Nothing we can't handle, but it does make this project a little bit different from what you're used to working on. We've been given a deadline, which I'm sure you'll have no trouble meeting. But if we miss the deadline we lose a lot of money, and more important to me, a lot of credibility. I want everyone to know how diverse we are. I want all hands on board to bring this project in on time and in grand style."

I looked at Carrie.

"Manuel 'Manny' Rivera, the publisher of *Latina Woman,* has contacted another firm, a Latin firm," Carrie went on. "His daughter, Esmeralda, was the person who contacted us and asked for you, Choice. She said that she was familiar with your work."

"Her father didn't like my work?" I asked and Dany laughed out loud.

"Mr. Rivera thinks your work is too sexy," she said. "I told him you could tone it down a bit."

"I'm not used to having clients tell me what or how to shoot."

"Still, his daughter is firmly behind you," Carrie reminded me. "Esmeralda thinks you make women look beautiful."

"I can show her father other work," I offered.

"We already did that," Carrie said.

"What more does he want? A song and dance?"

Curtis laughed out loud.

"Not a song, Brother Man, but you will have to dance. That's where I come in."

"Me? Dance? I have two left feet."

Curtis said, "Ladies, as you can see, my work is cut out for me, but I shall rise to the challenge and be victorious. NTA will have the Rivera account."

"What's going on here?" was all I could say.

CHAPTER 45

The NTA had to attend a party hosted by the Riveras and Carrie, Dany, and Curtis strongly felt that my knowing how to dance would help our chances of sealing this deal.

Curtis suggested that I come to his place so that he could give me a crash course in dancing meringue. I left my ride at NTA, thinking that it was easier if we both rode in the same vehicle, but wished I had followed him instead because on route to his house I had to listen to his philosophy on women, tattoos, and body piercing.

When we got to his condo I had to give Curtis his props, his crib was laid. In the living room were Crate and Barrels sofas and end tables, a stone fire place, thick carpet, smoked glass tables and large floor to ceiling windows. Although the cream colored furniture was sparse, they fit perfectly in the immaculate living room. It was like stepping into Tranquility. From the elaborate sound system, smooth jazz flowed throughout the room.

"Why do I have to dance?"

"Social graces, Choice. We've been invited to a Dominican birthday party. We're there to meet Mr. Rivera and Esmeralda but we're also there to show them that we appreciate their culture and hospitality. This is mixing business with pleasure, a common practice these days."

"But dancing has never been a pleasure for me."

Ignoring my every protest, Curtis put on some music and began teaching me how to do the meringue. After an hour or so of counting and dancing I got the hang of it, but I knew that I would never be comfortable on the dance floor. Curtis did commend me for trying though. But I had to admit to myself that I felt uncomfortable dancing with a man.

Afterwards, Curtis loosened his tie and brought out vodka and orange juice. There was no way I could keep up with him.

"Man, I got to get out of here. It's getting late, and I still have to get back to NTA to get my ride."

"I'll drive you back."

"I can catch a cab back to NTA." He had begun drinking heavily.

Curtis shook his head vigorously. "No, Brother Man."

We stood face-to-face like two gun fighters. I didn't want to shoot the brother down, but I was more than ready to go.

"I got to show you something," Curtis said as he opened a black notebook. "TWA, Choice. I want you to see this logo for my public relations firm: The Walker Agency."

Curtis had often talked about going solo, but the colorful logo he showed me let me know that he had moved beyond the talking stage.

"When is the grand opening?"

"Not in this area," Curtis told me as he put the black notebook on the couch.

"Does Carrie know anything about this?"

"This is between you and me, Brother Man." He patted his torso, looking for his car keys. I didn't tell him they were in the inside pocket of his jacket.

I sat down on the couch, hoping that Curtis would follow my example. I figured if I could get him to sit down, I could talk some reason into him.

"I won't be missed," Curtis told me. "I'm not her Golden Boy anymore. When I got to NTA, in the beginning, I was able to get anything I wanted. Damn, man, I felt like a King and Carrie was the Queen and Dany was the Princess."

I noticed the sadness in his eyes.

"I think Carrie really liked me because when I lived in Chicago I interned with the Burrell Communications Group; Carrie had a lot of respect for Mr. Thomas J. Burrell. Then later, before I knew anything about NTA, I worked for Mr. Burrell as a copywriter in his Atlanta office. I was in the ATL when I read somewhere that NTA was looking for a talent scout. I threw my hat in the ring. The rest, as they say, is history."

Curtis stopped speaking, as if another word would cause a flood of tears.

"I'm history, Choice. Carrie started her agency in 1971; I know she never had anybody better than me. Never, Brother Man. And I know she had high hopes for me."

I tentatively asked, "Did Carrie ever tell you she had problems with your work?"

"Brother Man!" Curtis shouted, startling me. "I'm nobodies' fool. I haven't brought in anybody. A few singers, a few artists, but none of them stayed. There was no way to recoup the money that NTA invested in their talent. They all got big headed and split. I felt bad, but Carrie said, 'Don't worry, these things happen.' Shit, man! These things don't happen to Curtis Walker! What the fuck, man!"

To calm him down I went to the small bar in his apartment got a glass, and poured some vodka in it, and then poured in some orange juice. He looked like he was on the edge of breaking down as I handed him the glass.

"What the fuck, man!" Curtis said, as he pushed my hand away, nearly knocking the glass out of my hand as some of its contents spilled on the hardwood floor.

"You don't get it, do you?" Curtis asked harshly. "You're Carrie's Golden Boy now. Even after all your fuck-ups."

"My fuck-ups?"

"Yeah, man. You know, your refusing to take pictures because the White models got a little freaky-deaky. You got an attitude and refused to complete the project. Carrie lost a grip on that one.

Then that calendar you were supposed to do for the Dominique St. Claire dance studio. That fell through big time, but Carrie kept that on the hush hush so that you wouldn't look bad. And she gives you the Rivera project on a silver platter. You fuck this one up and—"

"I won't fuck this up!"

"No, you won't because I'm on this with you. I'm going to show Carrie what Curtis Walker is all about. I'm going to show her that she didn't make a mistake with me; I just got some bad breaks, that's all. Show her that I'm the Golden Boy, then I will leave to start my own agency."

Curtis took the drink out of my hand. His tall body suddenly became lifeless as he flopped on the couch like a stone. "Yeah, Brother Man, she was really into me," Curtis said as he held the drink between his hands. "In the beginning, I even got the impression that she wanted me to hook up with Dany. Yeah, marry her daughter and inherit her company. But there was no chemistry, no chance for romance there."

Curtis guzzled down his drink, as if he was washing everything he said down. He placed the empty glass on the table near the couch. Then there was silence. Eventually, Curtis said, "I'll drive you to your car."

I didn't protest. He grabbed his jacket and pulled it on.

We drove to my ride in silence. When he reached NTA, Curtis pulled into the parking lot where I had parked. I reached for the door, hurrying because I couldn't get away from Curtis fast enough.

"Just a minute," Curtis called out to me. "This project is really important to Carrie, Choice. She wouldn't have been there at the meeting if it weren't. Understand that. Between you and me, Carrie is being considered for induction in the AAF."

"What's AAF?"

For a second I thought that Curtis would laugh at me and then kick me out of his car. "It's the American Advertising Federation, and it's a really big deal. Their convention is usually held at the Waldorf Astoria in New York City."

"You think that Carrie will receive this honor?"

"I have no way of knowing that," Curtis said soberly. "But I hear things. Carrie would love to have that honor. Anyone in the agency game would love to have that, and maybe someday I'll have it. But I'll never get it working for someone else. I have to have my own agency."

I got out of his car and walked over to my ride, and he burned rubber pulling out of the NTA's parking lot.

CHAPTER 46

The very next day, I met with my crew—Princess, Karen, Lydecker, and of course, Lorrie—at my loft, letting everybody know what was going on with our upcoming project. I decided to meet at my loft because I didn't want anyone at NTA looking over my shoulder. With this project I wanted everyone to know that I was the man to watch. When I handed in my work I wanted everyone to be stunned by my creativity and professionalism.

When we finished our meeting, I ordered pizza and Snapple for everybody. After they left, Lorrie hung around to help me clean up. There wasn't much of a mess to clean up so we spent the rest of the afternoon talking.

"I think she's stressed out. But she won't admit it. With D, everything is all right."

"Stressed about what?"

"Her career. Now that Dominique's dance studio is closed and Dominique's off somewhere in Paris, D is a free agent. Like me. So we have to make our own hustle; me with the makeup thing and D cries about having nothing. But that's not true. D has a lot going for herself. She's an excellent dance instructor."

"She can't see that?"

"She wants something big and bold and spectacular."

Lorrie walked around the loft, moving toward the back where I had a lot of my new photos. "Tell me about your work."

"What's to tell?"

"Why do you like taking pictures of naked people?"

"In my business, we call them nude studies."

"It still comes down to pictures of naked people," Lorrie said teasingly.

I was glad to see that she had brought her sense of humor with her that afternoon. I knew that talking about Debrena made our time together tense. I welcomed anything that would lighten the mood.

"I really appreciate you coming in on the Rivera project," I told Lorrie, "and sharing all your good ideas."

Lorrie smiled broadly. "Thanks, Choice. This gives me a chance to do what I love. And get paid for it."

"You're doing a lot. But I have to ask you to do a little more."

Lorrie looked puzzled.

"I want you to teach me to dance meringue."

Lorrie laughed. "Is that all? I thought it was something major."

"It's major for me. It may be the thing to seal this deal."

"Well, we've got to seal this deal so I can get paid. Give me your hands, Choice."

Lorrie grabbed my hands and taught me some basic steps. It was similar to what Curtis had shown me, but with Lorrie, a professional dancer, it was more about feeling than counting.

"I can show you even more if we had some music," Lorrie said as she went over to the entertainment system and found a Spanish station. We had to listen to a few minutes of Spanish mixed with English before any music came on. When the music filled the room she danced all around, her body moving smoothly in time with the music. She laughed out loud when she slid into some fancy, quick footwork.

"Now I know you don't expect me to do all that."

Lorrie laughed again, obviously enjoying the way she was using her body. "No, Choice. I was just showing off a little bit, letting myself go. It's been a long time since I've danced. I didn't realize how much I missed it. What I want you to do is this. Remember, men love to lead. Just stick with the basics and you'll be fine."

That was when Lorrie grabbed my right hand and placed it on her waist as she placed *her* right hand on my shoulder. We held our free hand together and she pulled me into her, but there was some distance between our bodies. Moving with her like that I really felt I was doing something, really feeling the music and dancing. We became so comfortable with each other that I moved closer to her body and her sweet smelling perfume put me in a rhythmic trance. Its scent brought me back to the night we once shared.

I didn't understand the lyrics, but the hard sound of the drums took control of my body. I didn't care how silly I looked or off beat I was. We got lost in the mood and the power of the dance.

That's the only way I can explain what happened next. Lorrie's body and perfume overwhelmed me as I moved in closer, pressing my body against hers. I'm sure she felt my manhood rising against her inner thigh. She didn't pull away. I moved my hand from her waist to the middle of her back and pulled her even deeper into me. I leaned in to kiss her. She moved toward me, her eyes unblinking on my eyes.

Then she placed her hand on my chest, preventing our lips from touching.

"We can't do this," Lorrie said apologetically. "I can't do this. I'm sorry. I have to go."

I held onto her because I wanted to apologize, but the words just wouldn't come.

"Lorrie, I—"

She was out the door, and I cursed myself for being a typically stupid male.

CHAPTER 47

Curtis and I had the honor of being seated at the Rivera table. The table was long and broad and covered with a white cloth, with the strings of floating balloons tied to party favors so they wouldn't float away. My eyes kept sweeping the large hall, filled with adults and children having fun and speaking a language I could never quite understand.

The beautiful olive to deep brown skinned Dominican women wore black, gold, and blue. Most of the men were dressed in white jackets, white shirts, and black pants like Manny Rivera. Manny continued a running commentary that included a lot of laughter and attention to the birthday boy, who was his nephew, and all the other family members who were his guests.

The dance floor was filled with fancy male dancers twirling their female partners and the children making up crazy moves that amused them and made the adults laugh. The popular meringue music was non-stop as the DJ made announcements in Spanish and then translated in English.

The Dominican Republic flag was prominently displayed as a back drop behind the Rivera table. Curtis saw me studying the flag and felt it was his duty to enlighten me.

"I did some research on that flag," Curtis began.

By that time, late into the afternoon, I felt we had been there long enough. We had eaten from a buffet that included chicken, beef, pork, beans, bread, rice, vegetables, and fried plantains. For dessert there was corn pudding and flan, and caramel custard.

"Do you know what the colors mean?" Curtis asked and smiled broadly when I shook my head. I would've said I knew just to shut him up, but Esmeralda Rivera was seated to my left and heard Curtis's question.

"How do you know?" Esmeralda asked Curtis in a soft Spanish accent.

"One summer I rented a cottage in Sousa, near Puerto Plata Bay." Esmeralda was obviously impressed. "I got to talking with a lot of the locals. I, like Choice, was fascinated with your national flag."

This conversation caught the ear of Manny Rivera who was seated next to Curtis.

"I was told that the colors in the flag stood for national pride and patriotism. Red symbolizes the blood of Dominican heroes. Blue stands for liberty and white symbolizes salvation."

Manny Rivera looked over at Curtis, clapped his hands, and said in a deep masculine tone, "Bravo!"

Curtis scored points with Manny and Esmeralda, especially when he engaged them in a discussion of key cities in the DR: Santo Domingo, Santiago, and La Romana.

Esmeralda smiled at Choice then turned to Manny and said, "Ellos estan tratando duro, de ganar nuestra confianza." *(They are trying hard to win us over.)*

Manny smiled, but what came out of Curtis's mouth caught everyone off guard, "No, yo no creo eso, yo pienso que es importante saber algo de la persona con quien uno planea hacer negocios." *(No, not really I just think it's important to know something about the person you plan to be doing business with.)*

When did Curtis learn Spanish? I thought.

Esmeralda said, "Muy impresionante." *(Very impressive.)*

"Pero no tan impresionante como lo que usted y su padre han hecho con la mujer latina," Curtis said. *(But not as impressive as what you and your father have done with Latina Woman.)*

I felt like an outsider and couldn't wait for this to end. My moment of truth came when Esmeralda invited me out to the dance floor. I felt pretty comfortable in the beginning, but suddenly the tempo of the music changed and all the coaching that Curtis and Lorrie had given me disappeared. I spotted Curtis across the room and he looked at me as if to say, *You can do it, come on, man. Don't let the team down.* Next to him was Manny Rivera who had a small girl in his arms.

I was ready to cut and run when two things happened: one, Esmeralda grabbed my hands and two, I began to remember some of the moves that Lorrie had taught me. I held my own for a little while, but began to sink and stumbled over my own two feet.

Curtis came to my rescue; he cut in and began dancing with my partner. He moved like a native, giving Esmeralda all the spins and turns that she wanted. He even made her laugh out loud as I faded into the crowd and became a spectator, clapping and urging them on. Together they looked like they were doing an exaggerated *Hustle,* a classic seventies dance, but with a lot of fancy footwork and upper body movement. All I could do was watch in amazement.

If only I had my camera, I thought.

"You did all right in there," I said to Curtis as we walked out of the club and into the parking lot.

"I had some private lessons. I did what I had to do to impress the client." Then he took a complete 360. "What's happening with you, Lorrie, and Debrena?"

"Nothing."

"After the throw down you experienced with those two? Nothing, Brother Man? You got to come better than that."

"The only business I have with Lorrie is when we do a shoot. There's nothing going on with me and Debrena at any level."

"I heard that. Sometimes these females are nothing but a distraction. You go home, Brother Man. Make your magic in that darkroom. You can't afford to blow this one."

With that Curtis slid into his car and finally left me alone. When I got home I checked the phone for messages. I can't say who I had expected to call, but I was a little disappointed that no one had reached out to me.

I thought about Lorrie and how her dance lessons had kept me somewhat afloat on the dance floor. I thought about calling her just to say, *Thank you.*

CHAPTER 48

I called Lorrie the next morning and asked if she would be willing to have lunch with me. I even suggested that I pick her up so that she didn't have to drive. I wanted her to be the first I told about the Rivera's party. It would also give me an opportunity to apologize for my behavior when we were dancing in my loft.

At first I detected some reluctance in her voice, but after a long pause she accepted my offer. I thought it would be best to go someplace outside of Elizabeth. I chose a fairly new restaurant in Cranford, New Jersey called The Office.

Lorrie stepped out of the house into the summer heat wearing off-white pants, a lime green tank top, and brown sandals. I was glad she didn't overdo it because I was just as causal with a pair of denim jeans, tee shirt, and sneakers.

On the way to the restaurant I told Lorrie all about the party and how I was able to use the dance moves she taught me on our client, Esmeralda Rivera, and how Curtis came to my rescue. Lorrie laughed as if she could picture the entire scene in her mind.

But then we got quiet. I actually preferred the silence as I turned on some music. A sit down discussion at the restaurant would set a much better mood for what I really wanted to say.

We sat in the back of the dimly lit restaurant at a table near a window. The waitress placed our drinks in front of us. We both ordered a peach Snapple and a glass of water with lemon. After the waitress took our orders she walked away, giving us the privacy I, for one, wanted.

"I've never been in here. It's nice," Lorrie said as she looked around the restaurant, admiring its ambiance.

"I've only been here a couple of times myself. The food is pretty good. Lorrie, I want to apologize for my behavior the other day. It was wrong and stupid of me. I was way out of line."

Lorrie gave a half smile. "You don't have to apologize, Choice. To be honest, I wanted to kiss you, but then I got scared. Lately I've been dealing with some serious emotions of my own. At one time I was always telling D how she was afraid of what she truly was and confused. Now I feel like I'm in her shoes."

She released a deep sigh and said, "The *Latina Woman* project will be my last project with NTA."

"Is this because of what I did in my loft?"

Lorrie smiled, admiring my guilt. "This has nothing to do with you, but everything to do with me. I need to find myself again."

"Does Debrena know all of this?"

"Me and D don't communicate much anymore. She's become a different person and so have I."

"You know when I hired you my intention was to somehow try to use you, in some sick way, to get Debrena back. I don't know if it was male ego or not, but I just thought what me and her had was something special. Now I don't know what to think anymore. Before the *Urban Vibe* shoot I went out to L.A. for a few days. When I returned home I saw you and Debrena at the airport." Lorrie sat up and gave me her full attention.

"You were helping her with her bags. Together you looked very happy, like nothing else mattered in the world as long as you had each other. And I couldn't resist. I had to take some photos.

I'm a photographer. I capture moments people think are meaningless. But to me these moments are filled with emotions that define who we are.

"I'd like to give those photos to you. I don't have any use for them. Besides, I have the negatives." And we both found humor in that.

CHAPTER 49

After lunch Lorrie agreed to stop by my loft so that I could give her the prints. As we stepped inside Lorrie sat on the couch and placed her purse down beside her.

I walked passed Lorrie and said, "Give me a minute. I have to get the prints out of the darkroom." As I was making my way to the darkroom my phone began to ring. I answered the phone, but once I heard the voice on the other side I became alarmed as if I was doing something wrong. Or was I?

"Debrena?" I looked over at Lorrie, but she didn't indicate that she wanted Debrena to know she was with me. I tried my best to put on a front. "What's going on? I was on my way out. You're outside?" Lorrie looked surprised. "Okay, give me a minute."

Lorrie stood and asked, "What does she want?"

"I don't know."

"Choice, I don't want to talk to her."

"Why don't you wait in the darkroom until she leaves? I'm sure neither one of us needs any additional drama in our lives."

Once Lorrie was in the darkroom I opened the front door and invited Debrena inside. She was stunning as usual, wearing a pair of designer jeans with no belt, a white tank-top, Chanel sandals and Chanel sunglasses. She wore very little jewelry, just a bracelet on her left arm and a watch on her right. But the way she wore this simple outfit made my hormones do summersaults.

She removed her sunglasses and released a deep sigh.

"Is everything all right?"

Debrena walked pass me and into the loft. I closed the door behind her. "We have to talk." Debrena said as she turned and suddenly faced me.

"What's up?"

"I don't know where to begin."

I moved away from the front door and walked further into my loft. Debrena seemed nervous, scared even as she tried to find her voice. "I…I'm sorry."

"For what?"

"Everything. I lied to you. I lied to Lorrie. I led you to believe that we would be together again, but we can't. What we had was good, but it's the past. And I lied to Lorrie because she scared the hell out of me. She told me she loved me and I knew she really meant it. That's why I set this thing up between you and her."

"Why, Debrena? Some people would kill for a love like that, a true love."

"The responsibility, Choice. If I accept that love, I'd have to change so much. I had to be totally true to Lorrie like she is totally true to me. I don't know if I can be consistent like that. If I changed that much, who would I be? I can't be only with a woman for the rest of my life. That's not me."

"Something really is wrong with you. You can't just go around playing with people's feelings."

There were tears in Debrena's eyes. "Lorrie gave you her body because I asked her to, and that was selfish of me. I shouldn't have pressured her to do that. But I can't take that back now."

"Have you shared this new found information with Lorrie?"

"No. I've been trying to reach her. I think she's ignoring me on purpose. Have you heard from her?"

Then there was a lump in my throat. I shook my head.

Debrena stood as still as a statue and let the tears flow down her beautiful face.

I couldn't believe this Kid and Play game Debrena had me in.

Was I supposed to feel sympathy for her? My first reaction was to jump her as if she was a man. But then I felt sorry for her.

When she finally found her voice she asked, "Can I please have something to drink?"

"No, problem. What would you like?"

"Water is fine."

I left Debrena alone in the living room to get her a glass of water. I didn't know how I was going to get her to leave, but I had to think of something. I didn't want to be in the middle of any lesbian drama.

When I returned Debrena was gone, but I noticed Lorrie's purse sitting out on the table. I hadn't seen it there before.

CHAPTER 50

Lorrie

Choice dropped me off at home, and gave me the photos he had taken of me and D. During our drive he didn't speak much. I'd asked what D wanted. He told me that she wanted to apologize for putting us in this situation and that she had been trying to reach me. Of course I had gotten the messages from my mother that she called. But I wasn't ready to talk to D.

I felt a little guilty, like I was cheating on D with Choice. It was an absurd idea but I couldn't shake the fact that Choice and I were leaving D in the dark. I felt real bad that she might have seen my Chanel wallet, the present she had given me, in Choice's loft.

Getting back into my daily routine would give me some balance because the way I was dealing with Choice had thrown me completely off. What was I doing with this man? Surely nothing could come from my involvement with Choice. My mind, body, and soul belonged to D.

As I entered my mother's apartment I could hear the TV playing in the living room.

"Your supper is in the oven," my mother said.

"I'm not hungry."

She looked at me with concern. "You have to eat something."

"I will." I sat on the couch and placed the envelope with the photos on the table. "I just don't know what I want right now."

I watched as my mother moved slowly to her recliner in front of the big screen TV. "You want to see something on TV?" she asked as she picked up the remote.

"I'll watch whatever's on," I said as I sunk deeper into the couch. I was so distracted that, although I was in the same room with her, I had no idea what was on TV nor did I really care.

I got up and went into the bathroom. After I washed my face, I looked in the mirror. But I couldn't shake the feeling that something was different about me, that something major had changed in my life.

I went to NTA for a new career and found myself on the rocky road to a new life. I was so excited and so confused. The sex with Choice was like nothing I had ever experienced before and it wasn't just because I had never been with a man; I had heard so much from D that I had a pretty good idea what that was all about. But what I had gotten into with Choice went beyond anything D had ever shared with me.

"Someone called a few times," my mother said to me once I walked back into the living room.

"Some one?" Suddenly I became tired, like all that had happened today had finally caught up with me. I had to actually fight the depression that threatened to pull me down. A little catnap might be what I needed. "Who called, Momma?"

"I made a note," my mother said as she dug into the pocket of her oversized housedress. "You know my memory ain't what it used to be."

Ever since her stroke, my mother left very little to her memory. There were even times when she greeted me at the front door with scraps of paper, filled with things she wanted to discuss with me. Sometimes the things she wanted to share, and was afraid to leave to memory, would be as simple as what happened on a TV soap opera or what she thought would be an interesting topic for a mother and daughter conversation.

I felt a little sorry for her as she handed me a pink slip of paper. I felt that her life should be more than sitting in front of a TV all day, cooking our meals, and taking messages for me. But she never complained. My life was becoming so complex, maybe her simple life held its own rewards.

"It was a girl who called," my mother told me. "I do remember that."

"Thank you, Momma," I said as I unfolded the pink paper. It was D again.

CHAPTER 51

Choice

The next morning Lorrie was late for the *Latina Woman* shoot.

"Has anybody heard anything from her?" I asked my crew as Curtis walked into the open area we were using at NTA.

"You hear anything from Lorrie?" Curtis asked Dany as she stepped into the area.

"Nothing yet," Dany told Curtis, then looked over at me.

I turned away from her and spoke to my crew. "I just hope Lorrie didn't forget that we're shooting here and not at the loft."

"I can't see Lorrie doing something air-headed like that," Princess said as she moved around the set she had put together. It was a simple construction, but it gave the room the feel of a small Spanish café where people came to dance on the weekend. I was pleased with what she had put together; I was also anxious to start.

"I can get a last minute replacement," Dany said as she stood near my shoulder.

"I'm sure you can, but let's not give up on Lorrie."

Did Lorrie oversleep? I asked myself.

"Are the models here?" I asked Karen, who was standing at the far end of the work area.

"They're all here," Karen said.

I knew we could do the shoot without Lorrie, but I felt her input would make the photos leap off the page. Because I was on a time deadline, I decided to go with a simple setup; the models would dance around in the clothes that Karen and Princess had picked out for them: swaying chiffon dresses, slinky satin dresses with jagged hemlines, flowing skirts with embroidered ballerina tops. Along with the fabulous clothes were earrings, rings, bracelets, and sexy sandals. The designers for the clothes included Oscar De La Renta and Carolina Herrera.

My plan was to combine action shots with fashion glamour shots, to have the models move, but look beautiful at the same time. I even had Lyedecker put some special lenses on my camera so I could get some dramatic wide shots.

Lorrie, Lorrie, come on, baby, I silently chanted. She was only fifteen minutes late, but because of the shoot being at NTA I couldn't create the relaxed atmosphere my crew was used to working in.

"Any music, Choice?" Lyedecker asked as he approached me. "You got a CD you want me to put on?"

I went to my camera bag and pulled out a CD. I handed it to Lyedecker. It was a mix CD of Spanish music, primarily for the meringue, a Tobias A. Fox master-mix, that included music by Elvis Crespo, Toni Rosario, Banda X, Zache, K-Libre, and Nueva Era.

Dany looked at me and I looked away again; I could even imagine her going to her mother and telling her how I had no control over my crew. *Lorrie, shit!* I said to myself, trying hard not to show my agitation. I didn't want Dany to say anything to me because I knew I would jump into a defensive mode.

"Sorry, I'm late," Lorrie yelled out, her black makeup case tucked under her arm.

"Let's get this show on the road," I said to no one in particular as I walked toward Lorrie. "You okay?"

Lorrie gave me a smile that touched her mouth, but did not reach her eyes. "I had a visitor."

"You want to tell me about it?" I whispered.

"Can we talk later? After the shoot? At lunch?"

"Yeah," I said, as she rushed past me to get to the models.

I turned around and found Curtis staring at me.

CHAPTER 52

ebrena paid me a visit this morning," Lorrie told me as we
sat in The Office. We shared a plate of veggies, a free
appetizer, as we waited for our main meal.

"You want another beer?" I asked. We drank Heineken out of
dark green bottles.

Lorrie smiled. "Two before lunch is my limit."

I smiled back.

"I was packing my case when the doorbell rang. I ran downstairs because I didn't want to disturb my mother. She doesn't
always sleep so well, and when she does finally get to sleep I like
her to sleep as long as she can."

"What did she want?"

"It's hard to say. D can be mysterious at times."

"You two talked, right?"

"I wouldn't call it a conversation. It was more like D talking
at me, doing a brain drain on me, getting everything out in front
of me."

"What did she have on her mind?"

"She talked about fidelity, being true to one person."

I had to laugh. "This coming from Debrena?"

"It floored me, but she was serious, Choice. I didn't want to
cut her off because she was speaking from her heart, but it could-
n't have been a worst time for me; I was trying so hard to be on
time for the shoot."

"Debrena was talking about being true to you?"

"Not so much to me, but fidelity in general, like a concept. What it meant and how folks should go about it."

"It just sounds strange coming from Debrena, especially now. I thought she wanted to play the field, not settle down."

"That's what I thought, but then she began talking about how it wasn't good to grow old alone."

"Maybe Debrena had a rough plane trip during her flight from L.A. Sometimes when there's turbulence you think about dying and all the things you took for granted."

"D didn't say anything about a bad plane ride. It was like she was checking to see if I was still in place, if she could still count on me to be a part of her life. I've never seen D so vulnerable." Lorrie took a long pause, "I think D suspects me of seeing someone behind her back."

I envisioned Lorrie being with someone else and Debrena chasing behind Lorrie, and me somewhere in the middle. I felt like I was the odd man out, and I had no idea how to get back in, or even if I wanted to get back in.

"You know, Choice, the biggest fear of anyone getting into a threesome is that their mate may start seeing that other person without them knowing about it."

"I can understand that, but none of that applies to me, you, and Debrena."

"No. It doesn't."

We stopped talking, digesting what had been said. Even though Lorrie seemed lost in thought, she was still smiling. "You seem to be in a pretty good mood."

"I was thinking about my mother, and how good she's doing."

I knew how suddenly parents could disappear. "I take it she's doing better?"

"She's doing much better. That's what's so great. Her doctor told her if she continues to eat right, exercise, and take her meds, she should be A-okay."

"That's good news, Lorrie."

"I thought I was going to lose my Momma. I was there when she got sick. It was a minor stroke, but it still scared the hell out of me. I was in her apartment watching some music videos when I heard her hit the floor. She hit the floor so hard I swear the whole apartment shook.

"I helped her to her feet and noticed that her eyes were glassy and she kept talking about how thirsty she was. She wanted to play the whole thing off, but I wouldn't have it. I nearly carried her out of the apartment in her housedress and drove her to the hospital. I raised so much hell in the ER that they saw her right away."

There were tears in Lorrie's eyes.

"They kept her in the hospital for a few days for observation. She's doing much better now."

"That's really, *really* good news, Lorrie."

"What about your parents, Choice? You never talk about your parents. What's up with that?"

CHAPTER 53

This was when I usually changed the subject, but Lorrie had shared so much personal information about her mother that I felt I should reveal some things about me

"They were murdered, Lorrie," I said soberly. "In the summer of 1982."

Lorrie didn't blink or turn away like I thought she would. This encouraged me to go on.

"My parents were part of this artistic community in L.A.," I began and suddenly wished I had some music on, anything to shield me from the harsh reality of my history. "They were always taking in strays, especially stray artists. Artists who had lost their 'mojo' as Lucky, my dad, always said. But there was this one guy. I never liked him, he always smelled of weed, and I never thought he was that good of an artist. He painted abstract nudes, usually women, but so abstract that you couldn't be sure what you were looking at. The only clue was the names he gave his paintings. The Red Lady. The Blue Lady. The Scarlet Lady. Queen, my mother, thought he was a genius. She organized his first showing within the community and asked Lucky to frame the artist's work.

"He called himself Tony DuBois, but no one thought that was his real name. He was the most unsophisticated man I have ever met. But Queen thought DuBois was all that. She even defended him when things began missing. You see, before DuBois showed up, no one had to lock their doors. But after he arrived things seemed to just disappear. He was never caught, but there was a lot of suspicion. Lucky and Queen argued about DuBois, until eventually, Queen left to stay with friends.

"That's when I began to hear bad things about Queen. Some people said that she was living with DuBois. I never saw them together though, and when I did see Queen she never said anything about DuBois. But I knew she wasn't happy and that someone had hurt her. One day she came back to the house with her arm in a sling. She said she had sprained it, but she never told me how she sprained it. Then one day after Queen had been away for a long time, she just showed up. I was glad to see her and I believe that Lucky was too. I just knew in my heart she had come home to stay. I left them alone downstairs so they could talk. I was just a kid, but I knew they needed some privacy. I went upstairs to Lucky's music room to play some records.

"I wasn't up there long when I heard three shots: I knew they were gunshots because there were no cars around and the noise was right in the house. I fell back against the wall and sank to the floor. When I picked myself up, the house was so quiet. I went downstairs and found the bodies. There was Lucky, Queen, and DuBois. He had shot my father and my mother, and then turned the gun on himself.

"It took me a long time to piece it all together; no one wanted to explain something like that to a kid. By the time I was an adult I figured that Queen had an affair with DuBois, but she wanted to come home to be with me and Lucky. Queen broke it off with DuBois after he had pulled her arm so hard, he sprained it. He didn't want to let her go. The way I see it, because he couldn't have her, he made sure that no one else would have her."

"Oh my God, Choice. That's horrible. I'm so sorry to hear that," Lorrie said to fill in the silence that had developed between us. "Thanks for opening up to me."

I noticed a couple across the room preparing to leave.

The woman walked ahead of the man and they were very well dressed in professional business attire. The only thing that was out of place was their obvious age difference.

"Isn't that—" Lorrie began, but I cut her off with a sudden wave of my hand. I got her to be quiet, but I also knocked over a half empty bottle of beer in the process. I didn't need her to tell me that Curtis and Carrie were leaving the restaurant.

"Choice, you all right?" Lorrie asked as I tried to clean up the mess I made.

CHAPTER 54

I'm sorry," I said as I waved a waitress over to our table. When she came over I asked for extra napkins. With all three of us working together, we had a clean, dry place for our meal, which the waitress soon brought over to our table. I let Lorrie eat in silence for a few minutes before I said, "I'm just surprised to see them together. This seems more of a restaurant to take someone you're dating or trying to seal a business deal."

"Choice, they do work together. You told me yourself, they've been working together for years, long before you came on the scene. Maybe they had business to discuss and decided to handle it here instead of at NTA."

"I just can't see Carrie and Curtis having a meal together that's not business related."

"What's so strange about having dinner together?"

"The last time I was with Curtis, I got the impression that he was ready to leave NTA. You know, strike out on his own, start his own company, TWA, The Walker Agency."

"He can't do that overnight."

"He's probably trying to get back on Carrie's good side, so that she'll have his back if he needs some kind of recommendation."

"What do you think they were talking about?"

"Who knows, probably me. My fuck-up today. Starting late like that."

"Choice, come on now. The shoot did start late, but once we got started everything went very well. I tell you, men are always competing with one another. Don't be so paranoid."

I smiled because Lorrie's comments did ease some of my anxiety. "I'm not being paranoid, Lorrie. You just don't know Curtis like I do."

"How did you get hooked up with NTA anyway?"

"I was in a group show in L.A. I had just left Eddie "One Shot" Gibson and I was trying to establish myself as a professional photographer. Carrie said she liked my work and wanted to see more of it. I let her see the little bit I had. Before I knew it, she's back on the East Coast and sending me a plane ticket, telling me that I was the next big thing, 'The Black Man Rising,' she told me.

"She got me shows in New York City, at the Lecia Gallery, the Metropolitan Museum of Art, the Brooklyn Museum, the Pace/McGill Gallery. I was her Golden Boy."

"With her going all out like that, you still seem insecure. I just don't understand why that is."

"There's always a lot going on in an agency like NTA. I'm not in all the meetings. I know that Curtis has a lot of meetings with Carrie and her daughter, Dany."

"And you think they're talking about you?"

"Who knows what Curtis is saying about me in those meetings."

"I think you're putting in a lot of worry about nothing."

"You may be right, but I just don't trust Curtis Walker."

CHAPTER 55

I spent most of the next day working in the dark room. I tried hard not to think about Debrena or Lorrie or Curtis or Dany or even Carrie for that matter. It was the loud knocking on the front door that brought me out of my refuge. I opened the front door and found Curtis standing there.

"Did Carrie send you?"

"What makes you think that?"

"So you're telling me you just happened to be in the neighborhood?"

"I got something for you. Can I come in for a second?"

I stepped back to let him in. Because I only wore a pair of jeans, it was obvious that I wasn't expecting any company.

As Curtis stepped into the loft I noticed the faint scent of alcohol on him. I picked my tee shirt off the floor, pulled it on, and then took a good look at my visitor. He had a black portfolio case tucked under his arm. "This is for you," he said as he handed me the black case that was the size of a large pizza box. "A present."

Before taking the "present" I asked, "Why you drinking so early in the day?"

Curtis gave me a mischievous smile and said, "I had a meeting with a client. You know me, I'm always working."

I took the case and said, "It's not my birthday or anything like that."

"We want you to look good tomorrow afternoon, when you present your work to the Riveras at NTA."

"Who is we?"

"Me, Dany, and Carrie."

"I'm just developing the last of the shots in the darkroom. I hung up everything to dry."

"That's good, Choice. Getting everything out of the way, getting a head start on things. I guess that means you'll be at the party this evening."

"What party?"

"At The Office. Me and Carrie checked out the place yesterday and we liked it. Carrie is hosting a little get together tonight."

"All this planning went on in my absence?"

"You left so quickly after the shoot that no one had a chance to talk to you. You weren't the only one who slipped out early. Lorrie got in the wind too, a little behind you. I'm going to have a word or two with her. I'm not about to let a fine ass like that get away."

"Let me put it this way, Curtis. I don't think your Lorrie's type."

"And you are?"

I had to fight to hold onto my self-control. "You don't need to mess with Lorrie, man."

Curtis walked deeper into my loft, like I had given him permission to do so. With his back toward me, he asked, "Is there something I need to know about Lorrie? Something you're not telling me?"

"I'm just saying you need to look before you leap."

"Lorrie is a fine ass mothafucka," Curtis exclaimed. "And you say she's just a friend? Because I don't want to offend you behind your woman."

"Lorrie is not my woman. You really need to understand that."

"You need to take some of that bass out your voice, Brother Man. I'm just giving the lady a compliment. She's a fine ass mothafucka, and you know it. Every time I say something about Lorrie you get all salty with me. I don't know what your problem is."

"Are you finished?"

"Almost. That black portfolio is for the work you did for the Riveras. Bring it to the meeting tomorrow. I'll be there. Carrie and Dany will be there as well. We expect you there. On time. You read me?"

"Loud and clear. You sound like you're Carrie's Golden Boy again."

"I told you, I'm leaving NTA."

As Curtis wrapped his hand around the doorknob, he smiled at me. When he opened the door to let himself out standing in the doorway was Londa Newberry, looking pretty in a pink sweat suit.

CHAPTER 56

S urprise," Londa said. At her feet was a large, black leather bag. Her sneakers were so white they looked like she had just taken them out of the box. The pale pink of her sweat suit pants hugged her shapely legs and round hips. There was a band of exposed light brown flesh between her pants and a halter-top that was trimmed in white.

"I hope I'm not interrupting anything. I could come back later," Londa said when I made no effort to respond to her sudden appearance.

"Stay," I said, my voice sounding like a command. "I mean, I want you to stay. You're not interrupting anything." I gave Curtis a look of disapproval. "We've finished our business." I noticed the cabdriver waiting for Londa to give him the cue that he could pull off. On her signal, the cab pulled off from the curb and joined the merging traffic.

I moved pass Curtis to grab Londa's bag with one hand and her delicate wrist with the other, and pulled her into the loft.

Curtis's face softened when he looked at Londa. It was the first time he had seen her in the flesh.

"You're even more beautiful in person," Curtis told her as he extended a hand to her. "I'm Curtis Walker, with the Nelson Talent Agency."

"Choice has told me about you."

I stepped in to make proper introductions. "Londa, this is Curtis Walker. Curtis, this is Londa Newberry. Curtis was just leaving."

"What brings you to Jersey?" Curtis asked. "I mean, besides Choice?"

"I'm interviewing for the upcoming Bridal Expo at the Jacob Javits Center."

"Will you be staying around for awhile? We're having a small get together this evening. We're celebrating Choice's fine work for a very important client. You should join us."

Before Londa could respond, I said, "Thanks for stopping by Curtis," and then I opened the front door, wide.

"Right. I'm sure you two have a lot of catching up to do. I'll leave you two alone."

Curtis pointed a finger at Londa and smiled like he had just hit the lottery. "It was really nice meeting you. I really hope to see you before you leave. Don't let your man keep you from everybody."

Londa stiffened.

"My man?" Londa asked when we were finally alone.

I ignored Londa's statement and asked with attitude, "So, what's with this surprise visit?"

CHAPTER 57

I s that anyway to talk to your woman?" Londa snapped back. "Don't pay Curtis any mind."

"I hope I'm not imposing."

"You're not. So, how long are you in town and why didn't you give me fair warning?"

"I called and left messages, but you never returned any of my calls. I thought we were friends, Choice. What did I do?"

"Nothing. It's not you. I just been swamped with work and now everything is kind of winding down."

"Well, depending on the interview I should be out of your way in two days. I may leave sooner, depending on you." Then Londa said what was really on her mind, "I don't like being used, Choice." She stood there with her hands on her hips.

"What are you talking about? How did I use you?"

"I know where I stand with you, but you could've at least returned my phone calls."

"Look, Londa, it's obvious you don't need me in your life."

"What? Who are you to tell me what I need in my life?"

"Like you told me, you're a strong, independent sistah."

"So I don't ever need a man?"

"You have a man, Londa."

Londa laughed. "What? What man do I have? You tell me,

Choice. Do you know something I don't?"

"The last time I called you, a man answered your phone. At first I thought it was a wrong number."

"Are you talking about Leon? Leon Parker? That's the guy you met at the trade show. I worked for him." Londa sat down heavily upon the couch. "I'm being punished for that? What do you think was going on between us?"

"Londa, it doesn't matter. It's your life, who you date is none of my business."

"This is so weird. I know what you're thinking, with your imagination. You're thinking I was in the shower washing Leon's sweat off me. You know us Black bitches, jumping on every man we know."

"I didn't say all that."

Londa jumped up from the couch and got all in my face. "You don't have to say it! Ignoring me for weeks behind some misunderstanding."

"What was I supposed to think?"

"Not that, Choice! Not that I am screwing Leon. You weren't supposed to judge me like that. I took you into my bed because I wanted you, and no one else, because I love you."

Tears fell from Londa's eyes, but before I could console her she quickly went into my bedroom. I stood there speechless.

She loves me, but do I feel the same about her?

CHAPTER 58

Y ou came all the way from L.A. to tell me that?" I asked
as we both sat on my bed.

"Why do you find that so hard to believe, Choice?"

"You could've told me you loved me before I left L.A."

"I could've, but you probably wouldn't have believed me.
You'd think I was still recovering from the good sex we had."

"That would have crossed my mind," I had to admit. I know
I've said some crazy things myself after sex.

"We've been friends for years. I wouldn't want to move too
fast and become an enemy because things didn't work out roman-
tically between us."

"I've thought about that, Choice. That's why I knew I could-
n't tell you this over the phone or in a letter."

I sat silently.

"Choice, I'm not asking you to do anything you don't want to
do."

"I know that."

"I ran into Janis and she told me all about you and Debrena."

At that point I wanted to end our conversation, take a flight out to L.A., and deal with Janis as I should've a long time ago. No matter how hard I tried to avoid her she seemed to always appear.

Apparently, Londa ran into Janis at the Garden of Eden, an upscale club in L.A. She remembered Londa from the Boat Expo. Janis had introduced herself and, of course, the topic of "Choice" came up. Janis didn't hold back in describing my relationship with Debrena, along with the real reason we are no longer together.

Londa saw the anger on my face. "It's okay, Choice. You shouldn't be upset or feel less than a man about that. It's not like you knew Debrena was into women. Come back to L.A with me."

"I can't do that. I've worked too hard to get here."

"You've done all that you can here."

"I've only been here for two years, Londa. I've just begun to do some serious work."

"You can do serious work in L.A. I'll help you one hundred and fifty percent, you can believe that."

"Being with you like that is something I have to get used to."

"Come on, Choice. It's not like we're strangers."

"You're talking this love stuff now."

"I was hoping that *we'd* be talking 'this love stuff' together; unless you're still hung up on Debrena."

"There's nothing for me there anymore. She's in love with someone else, or at least that's the way they carry on."

"What do you mean?" Londa asked.

I told her everything.

Londa shook her head. "You don't want to get mixed up in anything like that, Choice."

"I know."

"I mean, I'm no expert on lesbian relationships, but from what you told me, Debrena and Lorrie have a special bond. You can't come between them, no matter how you feel about Debrena."

"I know that now, Londa. But I don't see how going back with you to L.A. will make everything right."

"I'll never hurt you, Choice. I'm all about you. I just want to see you grow as an artist and a man."

"I can't keep running from shit, Londa. I'm getting the feeling that I never finish anything."

"That's not true, Choice. You have many great accomplishments. I'm just offering you a better life. A life without all this drama."

After a moment of silence I said, "I don't know. I have to think about this. Let's talk about this later. In the meantime, can I ask a favor?"

CHAPTER 59

When Londa and I walked into The Office I noticed Carrie, Dany, Curtis, Karen, Lorrie, and Princess already seated, engulfed in laughter and conversation. Of course, all eyes were on my date. She was tastefully dressed, wearing a white, fitted, short sleeved shirt and a white skirt that flared at the bottom coming just below her knees. She also wore brown leather shoes with straps that tied around her calves and a wide brown, leather bracelet on her right arm.

No one, except Curtis, knew of Londa's existence.

As we approached the tables reserved for NTA I took the liberty of introducing Londa to everyone as my good friend from L.A. Even Lorrie seemed pleased as she greeted Londa with a big smile and friendly handshake.

Carrie stood with her drink in her hand and said, "Now that we are all here I'd like to propose a toast." Everyone took their seats and grabbed their drinks. "Lydecker had to pass on this one. He's taking summer classes at Kean University. Well, I just like to take this opportunity to thank Choice and his magnificent crew for always coming through for NTA. And to show our appreciation," Carrie turned to Dany and she handed her mother a handful of envelopes.

Carrie took the liberty of handing out the envelopes stuffed with a check to everyone involved in the *Latina Woman* shoot.

Curtis stood and followed suit. "I'd like to make a toast as well, if I may?" he asked, directing his question to Carrie, and she nodded.

"To Choice," Curtis began, "Who knows how to bring out the beauty in his photography which is also a reflection of the women he chooses to date."

I looked over at Lorrie, but she held on to that smile of hers and I wondered if everything was all right.

After a few drinks and a delicious meal, Carrie stood and said, "Well, ladies and gentlemen, I don't mean to be rude, but I have other matters to attend to. There's some new talent in town. A young female artist by the name of Addelis is performing over at Rae's Café in Rahway this evening. I promised the owner I'd stop by and take a look."

Shortly after Carrie left, Dany made a few phone calls on her cell phone and then said her goodbyes. Following Dany, Lorrie excused herself and walked over to the bar, leaving Curtis, Londa, Princess, Karen, and me at the table.

CHAPTER 60

Lorrie

I walked over to the bar to order another drink. More than anything, I just wanted to get away from everyone. For some odd reason I felt a little uncomfortable around Choice and his date, Londa, as if I was the "other woman." I felt me and D's relationship falling apart and I wanted to make things right. Although I wanted to spend some time with D, I decided not to disappoint anyone from NTA and attend the celebration.

She is definitely wearing that outfit, I thought as I glanced over at Londa. I felt a little underdressed in my jeans, sandals, and fitted short-sleeve shirt. Seeing Choice moving on with his life made me want to reach out to D even more.

"Amaretto Sour," I said to the bartender.

While waiting for my drink Curtis walked up behind me, getting closer than I would have normally allowed. I put my hand in his chest.

Curtis smiled broadly.

"Excuse me," I said, but he just kept on smiling. He then noticed the waiter placing my drink on the counter.

"Let me pay for that," Curtis said as he dug into his pocket. "I'll have a shot of Hennessey," he told the bartender. He then turned to me and asked, "What's on your mind, pretty lady? When

I first saw you I said, now she is the hottest looking woman I ever met."

"Curtis, please. I think you had a little too much to drink."

Curtis ignored my statement as he paid for our drinks. I thanked him out of common courtesy. After he handed me my drink, he swallowed his down before I could even get a taste of mine.

I noticed Choice and Londa laughing it up with Princess and Karen. They looked really good together. Every time Choice would glance my way I would look away.

Curtis leaned in closer and said loud enough for me and a few others at the bar to hear, "Londa Newberry. That's a fine mothafucka there." He licked his lips. "She showed up on Choice's doorstep today. That boy ain't gonna ever settle down."

I leaned away from Curtis, trying to put some space between us and said, "I thought they were just friends. Platonic friends."

Curtis laughed loudly. "That's what Choice has been telling me for years. But this summer they moved out of that 'friend zone' big time. Choice went to Los Angeles and took care of business. I've been telling him to hit that for years; he finally did what I told him to do. I'm proud of my boy."

I found it hard to believe that Choice gossiped about his personal affairs and that he was so close with Londa, especially given how he got down with Debrena and me.

"What's the matter?" Curtis asked. "You getting a little jealous?"

"What?"

"I see how you looked at him during those NTA meetings, and during that shoot. How he looked at you. I know y'all got a thing going on."

"You're crazy. What makes you think I want Choice like that?"

"Come on, let's not play stupid. We're both adults."

Had Choice just been using me? Is he truly in love with Londa? If she's really his woman, how could he get down with me like he did?

I was so confused, my head began to ache.

"You okay?" Curtis asked. "You look sick. Look, I know about ya'll little secret."

"Excuse me?" I asked with much attitude.

Curtis leaned in even closer.

"I know about the threesome."

Curtis gave me a full detailed description of how me, D, and Choice got down with one another. He even stated that he would like in on the action.

"I know how to hit it right. Baby, I'll have you screaming my name."

"Choice told you all this?"

"Who else could've told me? How about you and Debrena taking me on in the bedroom?"

"That's a dream that will never come true, Curtis."

"Well, you know I don't have to have it like that. Just me and you, Lorrie. Now that would be da bomb."

"That will never happen either."

"Because of Choice? What is it with that nigga? He got skills like that? What he got? A fourteen inch dick?"

I turned to walk away.

"Wait," he said as he grabbed my arm. "I don't want us to get off on the wrong foot."

"I don't have anything more to say to you."

"Let me talk to you."

"You're wasting your breath."

"I want to get with you, Lorrie. I'll treat you right."

"Let go of me, Curtis."

Curtis held my arm, his grip beginning to hurt. I took my drink and tossed the contents in his face, causing him to release my arm and use his hands as a shield. I placed my empty glass on the counter and got out of there as quickly as I could.

CHAPTER 61

Choice

Here I was, sitting in The Office with one of the most attractive women in here, but I couldn't keep my eyes off of Lorrie, especially when she got up and walked over to the bar. I hoped I wasn't being obvious.

I would jump in and out of the conversation between Londa, Princess, and Karen. They weren't discussing anything in particular; just the basic questions about the history of my friendship with Londa, as well as her modeling and acting career, and of course, life in L.A.

After Lorrie threw her drink in Curtis's face everyone at the bar got loud and the commotion grabbed the attention of the customers.

As the manager approached Curtis I excused myself from the table and chased after Lorrie.

Outside of The Office I was able to catch up with Lorrie before she made it to her car. I literally had to grab her by the arm before she would talk to me.

"What did you tell Curtis about me?" Lorrie desperately wanted to know.

"What? What are you talking about?"

"You know damn well what I'm talking about!"

Lorrie broke it down to me.

"You're nothing but a selfish, egotistical male. I never want to see you again." She jumped into her car and quickly drove off.

I don't think there's an English word that could have described my anger.

I walked back into The Office and headed straight for Curtis, who was still at the bar, but this time running his game on another young lady.

I approached him forcefully and asked, "What did you say to Lorrie?"

"What? I don't know what you're talking about. And take some of that bass out your voice, Brother Man."

"You know damn well what I'm talking about!"

Before I knew it, Curtis was in my face. I pushed him, causing him to fight to maintain his balance. One knee hit the hardwood floor before he straightened himself up.

"What the fuck?" Curtis shouted. "What the fuck, man?"

"I don't like anybody in my face like that."

"Choice, don't you know I'll bust your mothafuckin' ass? Brother Man, you don't want to fuck with me. Lay your mothafuckin' hands on me again. I will kick your natural black ass. You can put money on that."

"Whatever. You need to relax, Curtis," I told him in a softer tone. "You're embarrassing the girls and you're making an ass out of yourself."

By this time, Londa, Princess, and Karen were on the scene and came between us. Many of the patrons were becoming concerned. The manager threatened to call the police.

I felt the best thing was for Londa and me to leave.

"You're talking all this junk to me because you think you're in a better position at NTA," I said to Curtis.

"Brother Man, you better start smoking some new crack. Instead of worrying about where I'm at you'd better check your position. One more fuck-up and you will be history at NTA."

CHAPTER 62

As we headed home, Londa tried to make conversation, but I was still heated over the confrontation I had with Curtis. I should have known better than to tell him about my personal affairs.

"Are you all right?" Londa asked.

"I will be."

Once we got home I headed in the direction of my sanctuary, my darkroom.

"Aren't you coming to bed?"

"I have some work to do. You go ahead. I'll probably sleep out here on the couch tonight."

"You can't hide in your darkroom, Choice."

"What are you talking about?"

Londa shook her head as if I just didn't get it.

"I saw the way you were looking at Lorrie. You couldn't keep your eyes off her."

"I'm really not in the mood to have this conversation."

"I'm here for you, Choice. I'll always be your friend," Londa told me and there was no denying the love in her eyes.

"Thanks."

With that Londa disappeared.

As I worked in the darkroom I thought about all that Londa had said to me. Still, I felt I owed it to myself to stay in New

Jersey. Carrie Nelson had done a lot for me and I felt I had to pay her back. As I saw it, the success of the *Latina Woman* project would be a big payment on that debt.

I couldn't stop thinking about Lorrie. I decided to give her a call, but only got her voicemail. She probably realized it was me calling and decided to ignore my call. Or maybe she was with Debrena, curled up in her arms.

I became exhausted and went to lie down on the couch.

When I opened my eyes it was 10:00 A.M.

I got up and went into my bedroom and realized that Londa had left. There was a note on my bed.

Choice,

When I went to bed, you were still in the darkroom. I thought you would join me in bed once you were done, but I fell asleep waiting up for you. I woke up this morning, alone, and found you out on the couch. I didn't want to wake you. I'm going to attend the interview today at the Jacob Javits Center and then I'm catching a late flight back to L.A. Remember, I love you and will always be your friend.

Londa.

I guess she was trying to make it easy for me by leaving like that, no awkward sentimental goodbyes, just a simple farewell letter. A *Dear John Letter* perhaps. It probably was best this way.

CHAPTER 63

I pulled my hair back and tied it with a long, thick black leather string. I threw on my white double breasted linen jacket and beneath it I wore a black muscle shirt with black dress pants. On my feet were my shiny black Martin Dingman shoes. I should've felt like a million dollars, but I felt like fifty cents.

When I reached NTA Dany greeted me at the front door. She smiled. I didn't have enough energy to smile back at her.

"We're meeting in the upstairs conference room," Dany told me. I held the portfolio case out to her.

"You hold on to that, Choice. We want you to make the presentation to the Riveras."

I nodded, but all I really wanted to do was hand her the photos and get back into my ride.

"We need to get upstairs, now."

I followed slowly behind Dany.

When we stepped into the room, Manny, Esmeralda, and Carrie stood to greet us. The Riveras looked tropical and colorful and Carrie looked stern and businesslike. Everyone was ready to get this business over and done with. I felt like a hired gun that had done his deadly work and had come to collect his blood money. I accomplished my mission, but I felt I lost my soul in the process.

All eyes were on me as I walked to the head of the table. As I untied the thick black strings that held the portfolio together, Carrie spoke to the room. "This is an historic moment for the Nelson Talent Agency and Rivera Productions. Mr. and Miss Rivera, we at NTA applaud your vision. Many years ago, many in the Black American community could not see us as beautiful as we are now. But there were others that knew that the image of the Black man and the Black woman had to be shaped and molded by future thinking people.

"When I began this agency in 1971, my desire was to portray my people in a positive light. With your magazine, *Latina Woman,* I see you are doing the same thing for your people, helping them to see themselves as beautiful, proud of their heritage, hopeful for their future. I applaud you both for that. I know that no one can do it better than you two can. I am just so happy that you have decided to give NTA this grand opportunity. I feel confident that you will leave this meeting with the best that NTA has to offer."

I opened the portfolio and looked down at the photos. My heart dropped down to my shoes.

"But I have said more than enough," Carrie continued. "Now it is time to hear from the man of the hour, Mr. Choice Fowler. Choice, please share your vision with us."

I slammed the portfolio shut and looked over at Dany. With a shaky voice, I said, "Could I speak to you for a second?"

Dany nodded, looking confused and scared.

"Outside the boardroom," I told her as she looked toward her mother, then back toward me. I turned to the others in the room. "Give us a moment, please."

I walked quickly toward the door, Dany following behind me, the black portfolio under my arm.

CHAPTER 64

hoice. Choice!" Dany called out to me, but I didn't stop walking until I was on the first level. "Choice, what's wrong with you?"

In anger I slapped the nearest wall, and then turned toward Dany. "Curtis fucked me!"

"What does Curtis have to do with any of this? You're talking crazy."

"Curtis wants to be the Golden Boy again. He can't be that with me around."

"What are you talking about?"

"I just don't know how he did it, Dany. How he got into my loft."

"Choice, you're scaring me. We need to get back to Mother and the Riveras. Let's deal with your differences with Curtis a little later, okay?"

"The only thing I can think of—"

"Later for Curtis."

"I can't go back in there now. Curtis fucked me over, Dany! He got in the last punch, the best punch, the knockout punch."

"Choice, give me the portfolio. I'll make the presentation. You go home. Do what you need to do to get yourself together."

I stood there half listening to Dany, trying hard to figure out how Curtis had sabotaged my efforts.

"We can't hold up the Riveras like this," Dany continued. "Just give me the portfolio."

"How did he do it?" I asked myself out loud as Dany stared at me.

Curtis must have made a duplicate copy when I gave him my key to look after my loft during my trip to L.A. "I'll be back," and headed to the front doors of NTA.

"What? Now, wait a damn minute, Choice!"

I ignored Dany as I walked out into the hot summer sun.

"What am I supposed to tell the Riveras and Mother?" Dany asked as we stood in the parking lot of NTA.

"Just stall them!" I pleaded. "I have to get back to the loft, grab up some contact sheets."

"There's no time, Choice. We're on a deadline. We have to deliver now! If not we lose the account!"

I grabbed Dany by her shoulders, sensing that she was about to become hysterical. "I'll be right back, Dany! You have to let me make this right!" I shook her and just as suddenly I released her; Dany was not the person I wanted to do harm to. My heart pounded in my chest like a drum.

"You're going to blow this for us," Dany said softly, pulling herself together. She had a lot of disappointment in her voice.

"I'll be back," I told her. "I'll be right back."

I ran to my ride with the portfolio under my arm. I threw the portfolio into the open window, on the passenger side. As I walked around to the driver's side, Curtis pulled into the parking lot.

Curtis parked and got out. He wore a white three piece suit. He saw me and smiled like the winner he knew he was. While I slept the sleep of the dead he had entered my domain and took out the photos for the Rivera project and replaced them with pictures of Londa.

Feeling I had nothing to lose, I stepped to Curtis and unleashed the dragon on him.

"Brother Man," Curtis began, but that was as far as I let him get. I fiercely swung and punched him on the side of his face. This sent Curtis back, but he didn't fall. I quickly followed up with a solid right to his gut. I hit him so hard in the stomach that he lifted off his feet. "What...the...fuck...man!" Curtis exclaimed as he fell to his knees, gasping for air. He held his stomach with his right hand and tried to push himself up with his left. Once he straightened up I hit him again. This time I connected with the side of his head and opened a nasty gash above his eyebrow. He managed to hit me in the face, but I punched him harder, this time with my left fist in his mid-section. Grunting in pain, Curtis fell back against his car and blood flowed from his mouth.

"Stop it! Stop it!" Dany screamed from behind me. "Choice, have you lost your mind?"

"You think you're funny!" I yelled at Curtis. "So fucking funny!"

"What the fuck, man!" Curtis shouted and I hit him again, trying to take his head off with a blow that I aimed at his jaw. Because he moved away from me, I only managed to hit him on the side of his head. Still, my blow knocked him down.

Dany ran back into the NTA building.

Curtis lunged at me. I used both my fists to pummel his mid-section like it was a punching bag. Only his stubbornness kept him on his feet.

"What. The. Fuck. Man," Curtis said, breathing hard, moving away from me like he was an old man. His white suit was dirty and spotted with blood. He stood there with his hands on his side, no fight in him, but he wouldn't go down. I had beaten him bloody, but I felt no victory and when Carrie and Dany came out of the building with the Riveras behind them, I felt shame. Like a thief in the night, I ran to my ride and burned rubber tearing out of the NTA parking lot.

I needed to get as far away as possible. I knew better than to go back to my loft. The same loft owned by NTA. But I had to go some place. Some place where no one would look for me. *Some place safe,* I told myself.

CHAPTER 65

Lorrie

It was the constant ringing of the doorbell that woke me up. At first I thought it was a dream, but after I had completely awakened I realized it was real. Since NTA's gathering at The Office I didn't want to deal with anyone or anything in the real world. I was emotionally drained and sleep had become my salvation. But then I realized that if I didn't answer the door the visitor would begin ringing my mother's bell as an attempt to reach me.

I slipped on a pair of jeans and headed downstairs. When I answered the door I was not the least bit surprised to see D standing there.

"We need to talk," she said.

Still wearing those oversized shades, I thought.

D and I walked upstairs into my apartment. Once we walked into my living room D didn't hesitate to speak her mind.

"Why are you avoiding me?" she asked.

"I'm not. I just need some alone time. Some time to myself."

"But what about me?"

My doorbell again.

Saved by the bell, I thought.

I went downstairs for the second time to answer my door, but this time I was completely surprised.

"What are you doing here?" I asked.

"I fucked up."

I had never seen Choice look so wild, so desperate.

"Can I come in?"

I reluctantly let Choice inside and we walked upstairs to my apartment.

As I walked into the living room, D shifted her body and tried to straighten herself up when she saw Choice standing behind me.

"This is cute," Choice said bitterly. "Real cute."

"What do you want, Choice?" His long dreadlocked hair fell pass his shoulders, his black tee shirt was damp with sweat stains, and his pants were covered with spots of what looked like blood.

"What happened to you?" Debrena asked, her voice filled with concern.

"I fucked myself. I can't blame anyone but me this time." After a pause Choice said, "I got into a fight with Curtis."

D looked intently at Choice, but there was no fear in her eyes. "What did you do to Curtis?"

"You know Curtis?" I asked D.

"I kicked his ass all over the parking lot at NTA," Choice said.

"Why, Choice? Why?" I asked.

"He screwed me on the Rivera account," Choice snapped at me. "I realize now I hurt myself more than I hurt Curtis. This shit ain't got nothing to do with Curtis. It's all about the three of us. Especially you, Debrena."

"I didn't say or do anything to make you go after Curtis," D said, sounding defensive.

I looked D in her eyes and asked, "How do you know Curtis?"

After a moment of silence, D looked at Choice, then back to me. "I met him one day at Malika's Place."

Choice shouted. "You put him up to what he did to me."

"Just the opposite, Choice." D said.

"I don't believe you."

"I don't care what you believe. I'm not lying to you. Or Lorrie. Or myself."

"You fucked him?"

"Fuck you!"

"Been there done that. Why did Curtis come to you?" Choice finally asked a question I too wanted to know.

"For some Latin dance lessons. He told me that he was invited to a Dominican party and he wanted to show out. I taught him to dance the meringue."

"That was all?"

"I also asked him about you and Lorrie."

"You spied on us?" I spoke up, truly hurt by D's actions. "If you wanted to know anything about me and Choice, all you had to do was ask."

D looked away from me, embarrassed. "I know that now. I guess I knew it then, but even more now. I know you'd never lie to me, Lorrie."

"All you've done is *lie* to me." I turned away from her.

"I didn't lie about everything," D said to my back as I walked away from her to the other side of the room.

"So that was it?" Choice asked as he sat on the couch.

D stood next to him. "What else do you want to hear? Curtis was so jealous of you. He wanted to sleep with me. I led him to believe that there could be a chance of that if he kept an eye on Lorrie for me. I wanted to know if you were sleeping with my girl behind my back."

"I'm not your girl."

"I don't want it to end like this," D said to me and there were tears in her eyes.

"How can I be with you, D?" I asked, my voice shaky as Choice stood up from the couch. "You don't trust me. You don't respect me. You use me when it's convenient for your pleasure."

"I'm sorry, Lorrie. I'll never use you like that again."

"You're such a liar."

"I didn't lie about everything. I didn't lie about loving you; I love you, Lorrie. I want to apologize to the both of you," D said. "What I did was so selfish. I invited Choice into our bed because I wanted to find out how much power I had over you. It wasn't about sex, that's never been a problem between us."

"Why did you have to pull me into this thing with you and Lorrie?" Choice asked.

"I used you Choice. Just like I used Lorrie and Curtis. I was wrong, so wrong."

Choice looked like a madman.

"I always knew Lorrie loved me. I was never insecure about that," D continued. "I was insecure about me. Lorrie was giving her all and I was holding back big time. I didn't want to give my all and end up with nothing. I wanted to know, I had to know, that no matter what I did Lorrie would always love me. I felt I had to test her like Angela tested Marcy. That's why I brought you in, but everything just got out of hand."

"So here we are," Choice observed.

"I am so sorry," D said. "I hurt you. I hurt Lorrie. I hurt myself. I have to admit I was jealous of the little time that Lorrie spent with you. But I had nothing to do with what Curtis did to you. I would never do anything to cause you physical harm. You should know that. We have to let go of all this bitterness and envy."

Then D turned toward me and the tears flowed down her face. "Because I was so insecure, because I thought I'd lose you to the first attractive person that showed a real interest, I did what I thought I needed to do to hold onto you. Can you please forgive me, baby?"

I turned away.

"Don't leave it like this," D pleaded and gently touched my arm as I pushed pass her.

I wanted to say so much, but I knew if I said anything I'd find myself standing like a statue in my living room, crying my eyes out, waiting for her to hold me. The hardest thing I ever had to do in my life was ask D to leave my house.

CHAPTER 66

Choice

The whole thing had fallen apart.

Whatever the three of us could've had together was nothing, but broken pieces lying all around us. I wanted to run after Debrena and I wanted to comfort Lorrie. In the end, I walked out of the house and got back into my ride.

With the black portfolio under my arm I walked up the stairs to the loft. Once inside I walked over to the nearest couch and dropped my body onto it. I placed the portfolio beside me. My mind went blank. I had only been home for a few minutes and already someone was at my door. My first thought was that Curtis had come for his revenge. I stood and walked over to the front door.

Carrie Nelson didn't wait for any invitation; she walked passed me and entered my space.

"What's gotten into you, Choice?"

"Curtis set me up. He sabotaged my entire efforts of making this project work," I said as I closed the door.

"Just how did he do that?"

"Curtis, somehow, made a copy of the key—"

"This is nonsense," Carrie said. "Choice. I know what you think he did to you."

"He wanted to get back on your good side."

"What do you mean?"

"Curtis wasn't happy at NTA. He'd been planning to start his own agency. I'm sure you sensed that. I saw you two together, having lunch, at The Office the other day."

Carrie looked at me as if she didn't recognize me anymore. "Yes, we talked over lunch at The Office, but it wasn't about me getting Curtis to stay with NTA. If you must know, it was about me passing on contacts so that Curtis could establish TWA, his own agency."

I didn't know what to say.

"But none of that explains, or excuses, what you did to Curtis. We got him to the emergency room. It took ten stitches to close the gash over his eye. He'll be all right and he's not going to press charges. He calls it a misunderstanding between brothers. I wanted to know more, but he wouldn't tell me anything."

Someone had switched the photos, my mind screamed.

"Choice, we lost the Rivera account. I felt like we were a shoo-in for that account."

"It's my fault, I'm sorry," I said humbly.

"I accept your apology, but it's too little, too late. You have hurt the professional reputation of my agency. NTA is an agency I hope to one day pass on to my daughter. I know she will be more of a business woman than I've ever been; it's in the genes. So you see, I can't afford to let anyone destroy that. I had high hopes for you. I told Dany that you were one of the great ones, another Eddie Gibson."

"I am really sorry I let you down, Carrie."

"You let yourself down, Choice. You got mixed up in a lot of crazy things. You lost your focus. I didn't bring you out here to complicate your life. I brought you out here because, selfishly, I wanted to be a part of your greatness. You will achieve that greatness. I have no doubt about that. It just won't happen in this time or space."

Carrie stood in front of me and I looked up into her face.

"I wish you the best, Choice. But it's obvious that you still have a little more growing to do. You have trouble accepting the world the way it is. You want to change the world and you will. You will get where you need to go. I will applaud you the loudest when you get there. But unfortunately it will not, it cannot be with NTA. Choice, I'm going to have to let you go."

Carrie left me sitting alone in my loft, contemplating another bad summer.

EPILOGUE

I took a cab from the airport.

Londa told me that I would find the key under the welcome mat. I found it and let myself into her L.A. home.

My plan was to put my luggage into the guest bedroom and take a nap. But because Londa and I had been talking nonstop over the phone ever since I was fired by Carrie, I felt the bond between us was a little more than just friends. As a matter of fact, as I walked into Londa's house, I felt like the king of the castle. There was no way that the king would sleep in the guestroom.

Londa had given me the impression that she loved me and wanted me to be her man. I walked pass the guestroom and into the master bedroom. As I stood in the doorway I recalled the sex we experienced in this room, in her bed. I laid my bags down by the door as I walked toward the bed. I thought about taking all of my clothes off so that when Londa came in she would find me nude in her bed. Because I thought that might be a little too much I left my pants on as I sunk into the softness of Londa's bed.

In the process of making myself comfortable for my little nap, I knocked a pillow onto the floor. I thought about just leaving it there, but I didn't want Londa to think I was a slob. I positioned myself on the bed so that my upper body hung over the edge. I reached down to pull the pillow up.

I broke out in a cold sweat as I knelt near the bed. I tentatively touched the black portfolio that I had found. I pulled it out and stood with it in my hands. I placed it flat on the bed and untied the strings that kept it together. I opened it and found all the photos I had taken for the Rivera project.

Acknowledgments

Saying thanks can go a long way. You just can never remember everyone that helps you in life. So, if there is anyone that we are forgetting do not hold it against us. We would like to start off by acknowledging someone who has helped us take our professionalism to another level. We like to call her the Queen of nHouse Publishing, but she prefers to be called Nitonya Story. Where would we be without your managerial and computer skills?

Along with her are those who seem to go far beyond the call of duty. They are always calling or emailing us about an event or trying to find a way to fit Terry B. in the midst of whatever is going on. Those people are Rhonda Berry, Comico Hadden, and Tammy Leverett.

We would also like to thank Eli, Isaac, and Paula Dweck for being the first ones to carry our previous title, *Dancer's Paradise: An Erotic Journey,* in their family owned variety store, Gateway Cosmetics. We are forever grateful. Also, much love goes out to Adrienne, Nikia, and Dexter from Source of Knowledge along with Rocky Samani and Emily Mallay for their support and arranging book signing events at the Penn Station Bookstore. But we cannot forget Ernest and Tracey Wheeler for their support as well and arranging book signing events at their Creative

Impression Bookstore. All of these venues are located in the heart of Newark, New Jersey.

We would also like to thank Marcela Landres for her superb editorial skills, Professors Vince Wrice and Al Shorts from Union County College, and the Rahway Public Library for their support and allowing us to utilize their facility. Also, much love goes out to Daryl Harris and Jerry Mouzone from Nu Xpressions in Patterson, New Jersey.

Of course, there are those book clubs that allowed us to enter their private meetings to discuss our literary works or gave us a favorable review. They are Samantha Jiles from A Nu Twist A Flavah, Pamela Bolden from The RAWSISTAZ Reviewers, Dawn from Mahogany Book Club, T. Rhythm Knight from APOOO Book Club, Jenny, who posted our first favorable review of *Dancer's Paradise* on Amazon.com, and Heather Covington of A YOUnity Guild Book Club.

We would also like to thank the book club members of One Mind Many Voices: Kae, Tammy, Leticia, Iyesha, Wydiah, Shimese, Tahitia, Kia, LaToiya, LaKisha, Latasha, Paresi, and Mrs. Bailey. Eloquent Women's Book Club: Bea Bynum, Dr. Rosalind Doctor, Michelle Doctor-Lowe, Deadra Holman, Felicia Jackson, Francesca Jackson, Sandra Johnson-Powell, Diantha King-Baptiste, Marilyn Leggett, Donna Lowe-Alexander, Candice Martin, and Jenella Miller-Smith. Sunday's @2 book club: J.T. Keitt, Lorane Reid, Crystal Zuckerman, Angela Pruitt, and Cat Jagarnaut. FIRE (Friends Inspired to Read Everyday) Online Book Club: Retonya Lasley, Valencia Battle, Kanika Naylor, and Danielle Obeng. Lastly, we would like to thank Rachel Nicholas from Healthy Babies Project, Inc.

Terry B.
Newark, New Jersey
November 28, 2006

More

TERRY B.!

Please turn this page

for a

bonus excerpt

from

The *E* Collection

A New Definition of Erotica

COMING SUMMER 2007

Terry B.

A Love Journey

By Tobias A. Fox

The moon illuminated the sky on this cool summer night. The evening was coming to an end, we were driving in my car with the windows down, listening to cuts by John Legend, 112, Common, Usher, and Mariah Carey. My date seemed to be feeling Mariah's "We Belong Together," but I was contemplating my next move while tapping my fingers on the steering wheel.

"I really enjoyed our night out," I finally said.

"Me, too," Journey replied, breaking her concentration from the music to give me her full attention.

We smiled as John Legend's "Ordinary People" broke through the airwaves. I really did enjoy the movie and dinner, even though I was more into her than what was playing on the big screen. Next time, I would prefer dinner and a movie at my place. This way I could show her that I have some skills in the kitchen. Or maybe we could go out dancing at Club Cherries in Atlanta so I can see how she moves her body on the dance floor and show off my fancy footwork.

"We should do it again some time...soon," I said.

"I'd like that."

Thoughts were racing through my mind. We were back at my place, and I had to think fast. She had driven her car to my house, but we agreed to go on our date in my ride. Now we were both waiting to say goodbye. Looking at my watch, I noticed the time…12:25 A.M.

The night is still young, I thought.

We had learned so much about one another in just a single night. Journey Love, originally from Birmingham, Alabama, is the older of two siblings with aspirations of being something larger than life, unlike her mother and father. I saw sorrow in her eyes, even tears she fought back while telling me about her childhood. Understanding her pain, I felt compelled to tell her my life story of how I grew up in East Orange and Newark, New Jersey where it's overpopulated with drugs, crime, and gangs. The grass definitely wasn't greener on either side. As I saw it, we were a match made in Augusta, Georgia, where we now lived.

We'd met two weeks ago at the Cheesecake Factory. I bumped into her while she was coming out and I was going in. After our apologies and becoming somewhat acquainted, we exchanged numbers.

Common's song "Go" came on next and pumped me with courage. "Look, Journey, I really don't want this night to end just yet. Why don't you come inside?"

"Okay," she answered after a short delay in response. "I can stay for a little while."

I tried hard to keep my composure and be the perfect gentleman. They say the first impression is a lasting impression, so you should make it the best, which is what I was aiming to do. At the end of this night, I didn't want to have to worry about whether or not I would hear from her again.

After making our way to my front door and stepping inside, Journey walked deeper into my place and entered the living room. I came up behind her and asked, "Do you want something to drink?"

"No," she answered while taking off the light jacket she'd been wearing to cover her bare arms while we were in the theatre. Her Chanel perfume quickly filled the air and stirred my emotions, like fuel to my fire.

Damn, she's gorgeous, was all I could think as I stood facing her.

"Can I get you anything?" I asked.

"No, I'm good."

"Would you like to hear some music then?"

"Sure," Journey said as she sat down on the couch.

I walked over to the entertainment system, hit the power button, and cued 112's "U Already Know." As the sound of the music broke the silence, I cleared my mind and thought, *What the hell.*

Walking back over to Journey full of confidence, I took her by the hand, pulled her up off the couch, and snuggled her close to my body.

"This is something I wanted to do all day," I confessed, and then pressed my lips against hers.

It seemed like we were kissing forever. We started out with small pecks, which led to wet, passionate kisses as our tongues danced. She occasionally sucked on my bottom lip and I returned the pleasure. The pounding rhythms of our heartbeats drowned out the sounds coming from the speakers. We were speaking a body language only she and I could understand. We were in a world of our own, letting everything go. Then I felt her body pulling back, and I followed suit as we came up for air.

God, I want this woman, I thought.

She was every bit of a woman, and not just in a physical sense. The way she carried and expressed herself assured me she had stopped being a little girl a long time ago, and that turned me on even more. What I like most about Journey, though, was she showed a genuine interest in me. She actually paid attention when I spoke, as if everything I said mattered. How could I just let her go? I wanted her. No, I *had* to have her.

"Let's go in the bedroom," I seductively suggested, trying not to sound demanding or controlling, but wanting to know everything there was to know about Journey's love.

I took her silence as a yes. After turning off the music, I took Journey by the hand and led her into my bedroom. Once inside, I didn't bother turning on the lights. Instead, I lit a candle and turned on my satellite radio, which was tuned to the slow jam station. As K-C and Jo-Jo crooned "Stay," I noticed the time on my digital clock…12:45 A.M.

It's still pretty early considering the night, I thought.

I turned to Journey, who stood by the door anticipating my next move. As I passed her to close the door, my body brushed against hers. I wanted to warn her anything goes behind this closed door, but I'm sure the expression on my face told her that I was going to take pleasing her very seriously.

The shadows from our bodies touched before we did. Our spirits connected. Our minds were in sync the entire evening. Now, it was time to find out how well we would respond physically to one another.

She wasted no time as she placed her hand behind the back of my head, pulling me closer to her. We kissed again, but this time with a heated passion I never felt before. Journey and I had become completely different people from just moments ago. It was like the soft music and burning of the candle helped set the mood for this love scene. However, there was no director, no script, and we definitely weren't actors.

As we kissed, we started pulling and tugging at each other's clothes. In the process, we stumbled into the wall, the door, and against the dresser, knocking over the contents sitting on top. We were acting like two drunken, lovesick fools. Yet, neither one of us had anything to drink. In that sense, we were actors, but everything we did was adlib, just going with the flow of things. We continued this wild dance until we were completely naked.

Our breathing was heavy, hearts racing as we stood fully exposed, facing one another. We no longer cared what was playing on the radio. There were no embarrassing moments. No awkwardness. No shame in our game. We knew what we wanted and how we wanted it.

Still, I had to make the first move to protect my ego, to feel in control of this intense situation. She must've sensed this because she complied and let me lead her three steps to my queen size bed.

"Do you have protection?" she asked.

I walked over to the nightstand, opened the drawer, and pulled out a pack of three...Magnum, of course. After stepping back over to Journey, we both climbed onto the bed. I lay on my back, placing the condoms by my side, and then pulled her on top. Journey thought I wanted her to ride me, but I had other plans. She looked at me strangely as I tried to pull her up further.

"I want to taste you," I said in a seductive whisper.

Knowing exactly what I was talking about, Journey crawled up my body and even *purred* like a kitten, but I knew better. I knew once she got open, she would become a wild alley cat. She didn't stop climbing until her bottom was above my face. As she spread her legs, her pussy smiled and I could see the moistness on her clit, aiming for my mouth. I licked my lips on cue as she lowered herself.

I opened my mouth and accepted all she had to offer. As I sucked and pulled on her clitoris, my bottom lip slid in and out of her. I looked up and saw that Journey had her eyes closed. Her head fell back, then to the side, and then forward, as if she had no control over her body. She licked her lips as she rubbed and stroked her breasts and nipples. She was in her zone, enjoying every sensual pleasure of having her clitoris stimulated.

She then became forceful, grabbing my head with both hands and riding my mouth like a go-go dancer giving a lap dance. All I could do was grab her waist, hold on, and enjoy the ride. Her juices flooded my mouth as she began moving faster, and faster, and faster.

"Come on, baby. Get this pussy. Get this pussy. You want it? Tell me you want it."

I tried responding, but the wider I opened my mouth the deeper she pushed herself in. I was drowning in her love. Suddenly, her body started jerking and tightening up.

"I'm…about…to…come, baby!"

Her words and reaction excited me. I even tried doing a little head movement to enhance her orgasm, but it was useless. She used my head like a sex toy. A flood of emotions overflowed my mouth as her juices ran down the sides of my face. Journey jerked her body back as she began moaning and screaming, creating a soundtrack of her own. She pounded her fist against the headboard before collapsing on my face.

She tried to regain her strength and composure while lifting up and sliding down onto my body. As I looked into her eyes, I saw tears flowing down her cheeks. Not knowing what to say, I said nothing.

"I'm sorry, baby," she said with all sincerity. "I needed that."

You really never know what one is going through, I thought.

Journey hugged and kissed me on the lips, but didn't stop there. She started kissing on my neck and chest, giving my nipples special attention, which really got me aroused. I arched my back a little and let out a deep moan of my own. Journey smiled as she continued teasing me, as if she liked seeing me in such a vulnerable state.

She moved down to my belly button and then put all of me inside her mouth, giving me some deep throat action. This caused my toes to curl and my back to arch more than normal. My mouth fell open, but nothing that came out made sense, only sounds. I grabbed onto my sheets as if I was on a dangerous ride and didn't want to fall off. Emotions were building up inside of me and a knot was forming in my stomach.

What's happening, I wondered.

I became scared and pushed Journey off of me.

"What's wrong?" she asked, sounding concerned.

"Nothing."

I had to stay in control. I didn't want to lose control.

"Lay on your back," I demanded, but my forcefulness only made Journey smile as she complied.

I put on a Magnum condom and climbed on top of Journey, whose legs were spread wide open. She was wet and ready. I slid in and out of her in slow motion at first, and then sped things up a bit. I lifted her legs, arched myself in a pushup position, and turned it into a workout session. After about a set of fifty, I put Journey's legs down, placed my legs outside of hers, and began climbing up the ladder. I pushed myself as deep as I could go inside her.

Journey kept challenging me to go deeper, faster, harder, and I tried my best to stay in the game. She definitely was picking up what I was putting down. She scratched the flesh of my back as she moaned deeply in my ear.

Pulling myself out, I said, "Turn over. I want it from the back."

Journey kept smiling, taunting and teasing my ego. She got on all fours, resting the top of her body on the bed while reaching back to spread her cheeks.

"Come get this pussy, daddy."

That I did. I slid inside her, gently pulling her hair and kissing her softly on her neck as I went in and out, in and out, in and out. She kept encouraging me, letting me know I was performing to her satisfaction.

"Come on, baby. Don't stop! Don't stop!"

I kept this rhythm going until Journey's walls erupted and there was an explosion once again. Her body collapsed on the bed and I rested mine on top of hers while still inside. I then got up and turned over onto my back. I looked over at the clock and saw it was 2:00 A.M. We had been going at it for about an hour strong. I smiled, proud of my stamina and self control.

"My turn now, baby. Get on top of me."

Journey used every bit of strength she had left and pulled her body on top of mine. She smiled, obviously impressed at how I was able to keep up.

"You gonna come for me, baby?" she asked.

I just smiled back.

Journey grabbed my manhood with one hand as she squatted and positioned herself. Then she dropped down and did The Eagle. She moved in a circular motion as she rested her hands on my chest. We moved in unison. Our bodies became one. We created a dance of our own. It was a dirty dance, a downright funky dance. We began moving faster, and I felt a tingling at the head of my dick.

"I'm about to come! I'm about to come!" I shouted.

"Yes, baby, let it go. Please, don't hold back."

I released everything I had in me. The emotions once built up inside of me returned, and so did the knot in my stomach. I couldn't hold back any longer. I had to release it all.

Journey leaned down and kissed me on my hot, wet face. I noticed a strange look on her face, as if she was holding something back but wanted to get it out. Then, tears started to fall from her eyes. However, she smiled and this confused me even more. It was as if she was sad and happy all at the same time.

"What's wrong?" I asked.

She leaned in closer and whispered, "Baby, you're crying. I never saw a man so emotional after sex."

Crying? Me? I never felt this emotion before. I never cried during sex. I felt embarrassed, ashamed. I tried wiping the tears from my eyes, but they wouldn't go away. I was crying for sure. And then it all poured out. I cried like a baby and held on to Journey as if my life depended on it.

ONCE YOU GO BLACK

By Terry W. Benjamin

Dear Hillary,

After it was all over I didn't want to get out of the bed. Even though we had gone at it hot and heavy that night, it still wasn't enough for me. I greedily wanted more, more, and more. To say he blew my mind is an understatement. With that man, that lover, the earth moved and the stars fell from the sky. The scary thing is I almost missed this opportunity by being my conservative self.

"I don't deal with conservative women," I overheard him say as I came out of the ladies' room. We were at a university-wide celebration and the administration went all out with the food and drinks. I walked pass him and a small group of men who were drinking and trash talking, like they had to prove that although they were intellectual men, college professors and administrators, they were still virile men that screwed women.

Blushing, I turned beet red because I knew he was talking about sex with a woman like me. Although I had eavesdropped, I knew the only way we could get together was if I changed my conservative ways and didn't block an opportunity for a most excellent sexual experience. But only if I were ready and willing to take that chance.

He stood tall and manly in his black tuxedo with silk purple lapels. I thought his tux was a little flashy for this conservative crowd. Because he was a young, black college professor, I couldn't expect him to dress or even act like the old heads that had been around when I was an undergraduate at Florida University where we both worked.

Since I got a lot of compliments from men and women on my peach and cream silk gown, I guess I wasn't looking too shabby myself. The gown swept the floor, covering my peach and cream silk pumps, and he almost stepped on the bottom of it as we danced to the music of the live band that consisted of undergraduate music majors.

He taught African American Literature and I taught Political Science. I never imagined we would even be at the same table, but because I decided to attend the banquet at the last minute, I had to sit wherever they could fit me in. I found myself seated at a table at the back of the banquet hall with him and Gayle Lord, a grad student in the Political Science department and current president of the African American Students League. Gayle looked extra special in a white silk gown that left her dark shoulders bare. The three of us engaged in some small talk until he decided to leave our table to speak to someone across the room. Of course, when he left, Gayle and I got our chance to talk about him.

"He's easily the best looking man in the English department," Gayle commented, referring to the young African American literature professor, as she sipped from her third glass of champagne.

I nodded in agreement, thinking about all the overweight and out-of-shape baldheads in that department.

"Possibly the best looking man at Florida University," Gayle went on.

I wasn't too sure about that because there was a senior professor in the Biology department who made my panties wet every time I stood next to him. His all-white hair and sky blue eyes produced a chemistry between us that neither of us wanted to acknowledge; him, because he was married and me, because I was too chicken to approach him in a sexual manner.

"Just look at him," Gayle said, awe and admiration in her soft voice. It was obvious that no matter what was taking place in the banquet hall, he was her main reason for being there. It was also obvious Gayle could look at him all night.

"He *is* very handsome," I modestly admitted, holding up my end of the conversation. I was somewhat off balance because I never dreamt I would ever talk to Gayle Lord or any other woman about him. I had known Gayle for years, but we had never had any extensive conversations, and here we were discussing the sex appeal of a young African American professor.

Should I encourage it and go with the flow? Or play Miss Prissy and shut it down as inappropriate?

"You'd have a better chance with him than I would," Gayle told me as a little bitterness seeped into her soprano voice.

"Why is that?" I had to ask.

"I heard he only dates white women."

With the attitude Gayle showed. I felt like I had to defend him, but I needed a little more information. "Who told you this, Gayle?"

"A sistah who ran into him recently at a party. She laid some not-so-subtle hints on the brotha, but he didn't respond at all. Then this white woman shows up and he practically runs to greet her. How ya like that?"

To me, that didn't seem like enough to label him a lover of white women exclusively. My feeling was that a man, black or white, who respected a woman made her feel special around him. All I saw him being was a respectable gentleman.

"He also doesn't like conservative women," Gayle went on, telling me something I had already heard from his mouth. I just wasn't sure what *she* meant by it.

"Conservative, Gayle?"

"In bed. Too conservative. Too uptight when it comes to certain things."

"Certain things like what?" I naively asked.

Gayle looked at me like I was crazy. "He likes his dick sucked and his balls licked. A lot of sistahs don't get down freaky like that."

"And he likes white woman because they do all that?" I asked, amused by such stereotyping in this day and age. I am a thirty-four-year-old white woman and before that particular night I had never licked any man's testicles. To tell the truth, I was afraid to touch them, stroke them, or fondle them, fearing I might hurt the man and it would be such a turn off that he would never want to have sex with me again. Whenever the thought of something "freaky" like that crossed my mind, I dismissed it because I felt the next thing my lover would want me to do was ream his ass crack with my tongue. And that was something a conservative like me would never do. It was like going where no man (or woman) had ever gone before. I had to shake my head and wonder where she got those crazy ideas about white women.

Gayle looked at me like she expected some confirmation.

"I can't speak for all white women," I told her, "but, Gayle, not all white women do those things in bed."

Gayle looked at me skeptically. "Suck dick, lick balls, and take it up the ass," she said as if to sum up the full sexual repertory of white American women.

I could've told her that I sucked cock, but never took it up the shitter. I always thought of my rectum as an exit, not an entrance. Maybe I was being too conservative in this new millennium.

"Are you uncomfortable with this conversation?" Gayle asked, obviously commenting on my sudden silence.

"It's not that," I assured her, groping for a satisfactory answer to her question. "I'm not uncomfortable with discussions about sex. It's just all this talk about sexual preferences may be a speculation, Gayle. I don't know him like that and neither do you… I mean, we don't know him intimately."

"I've heard a lot of things, though."

"Okay, but have you ever been there with him, Gayle?"

"I wish. I would let him tap this ass."

I couldn't help but to blush.

Gayle laughed out loud, a low sexy growl. That sexy low laugh seemed to come from somewhere between Gayle's thighs.

It was a cross between a moan and a whimper. The thought of such deep carnality pulled my thoughts away from the professor for a moment and had me thinking about the first time I did something sexual that I was totally unprepared for. And because I was totally unprepared for it, I didn't enjoy it as much as I could have.

Even though Gayle said black women were not his first choice I couldn't help but imagine the two of them together, screwing their brains out and sweating like pigs, their dark bodies on white satin sheets while her heels were up on his broad shoulders and his dark brown cock pumped into her tight, wet cunt. I had to admit Gayle had me thinking sexy thoughts about the professor.

"I bet he's got a nice, big, juicy dick, too," Gayle continued, obviously intoxicated from the champagne.

I was glad when he returned to the table because I didn't want to engage in any more sex talk with Gayle Lord, especially when I had come to the banquet hall alone and planned to go home alone. Why get my cunt all wet when there was no one to satisfy me? I could do the job myself, but I had never been a fan of solo sex. After an orgasm, I like pillow talk. You couldn't get that from a sex toy.

The evening came to an end with brief remarks from the president of the university. While making my way out of the banquet hall and into the parking lot, he called out to me.

"Diane," the professor called as I stood near my Lexus.

"Can I help you?" I asked, a lot more formal than I intended to be. I felt like I had to protect myself, to resist the charm of this black man who only bedded white women. Still, I blushed, my face hot because of my presumptuousness. Who was I to think he wanted me naked with my legs spread wide just because I was a white woman?

"You can *help* Gayle," he answered with a killer smile, brilliant white teeth, and healthy pink gums. "I don't think Gayle is in any shape to drive herself home."

"You want me to drive her home?" I asked, wanting to make sure I understood his request.

"That's right," he told me. "I want you to drive Gayle in your car and I'll drive Gayle's car. That way, Gayle won't have to leave it here in the parking lot."

"How did you get here tonight?" I asked out of curiosity.

"Public transportation. I had no idea I would be here tonight. The chairman of my department had some extra tickets; he gave me one for free and said it would be good politics if I showed my face."

I nodded, letting him know I understood all about departmental and university politics. I had many collegiate war stories of my own that I could share with him.

"Besides, as a new professor, I can't afford the luxury of a car."

I nodded again. I knew starting out on your own always contained some element of struggle.

We went back into the banquet hall and found Gayle in the ladies' room puking her guts out. Well, it would be more accurate to say *I* found her in the ladies' room, and he waited outside the door.

Gayle seemed glad to see me as she hugged the commode like it was a long lost friend. The miracle for me was she didn't get any puke on her gown. I helped her to her feet. Outside the ladies' room she used me and the professor as crutches while the three of us made it out to the parking lot. She handed the professor her car keys, and he followed behind me in her car.

Gayle rode with me, sprawled out across the backseat. Once we arrived at her apartment and settled her in the bed, we got back on the road.

"Where to?" I asked.

He gave me directions to his apartment and we were there in less than fifteen minutes.

"You look beautiful tonight," he expressed as we sat in front of his apartment building.

"Thank you," I replied, and then blushed.

"I know it's late, so I won't keep you," he told me while unbuckling his seatbelt.

"You're not keeping me from anything."

"I can't believe Gayle got blasted like that," he said, having no idea he played a role in Gayle's overindulgence.

"You had something to do with it."

"Me? How?"

"I shouldn't be telling you this, but Gayle has a major crush on you."

He looked shocked. "Gayle never said anything to me, Diane. We didn't even have any small talk until you came to join us. I just sat there in silence while Gayle drank glass after glass of champagne. You saw her; she didn't even touch her food. A crush on me? How could that be?"

"Don't ask me to explain it fully, but my guess is that Gayle finds you intimidating."

He laughed out loud. "Intimidating? Me? I'm a pussycat."

"That's the only way I can account for her shyness."

"So because she can't talk to me, Gayle drinks too much, gets sick, and embarrasses herself?"

"Like I said, I can't fully explain it, but that is my take on the situation."

He shook his head in wonderment as if to say, *I don't understand women at all.*

"Besides that, Gayle thinks you prefer white women over black women."

"Where'd she get that crazy idea?"

Then I was a little puzzled. "You don't prefer white women as lovers?"

"Diane, read my lips. I've *never* been with a white woman sexually."

"That's what Gayle believes, which is another reason for her to think she doesn't have a chance with you."

"Next, you're going to tell me that she believes white women are better in bed than black women."

I held up my hands in mock surrender. "I don't want to get into that debate. I have no field evidence to refute that proposition."

He smiled broadly. "No 'field evidence'? Are you telling me that everything can be proven by field evidence?"

"A lot of my distinguished colleagues swear by it."

"What about you?"

"I get a lot of good information from libraries and the Internet."

"But is it ever as satisfying as tracking down 'field evidence'?"

I found myself blushing and becoming aroused at the same time. I felt he was manipulating me and I didn't like that at all.

"Don't push me into a corner on this," I snapped. "I'm just trying to help you understand Gayle. Don't push me like this. I don't like to be manipulated in any way."

"Is that what I'm doing?" he asked defensively.

"I detect some not-so-subtle sexual probing."

"Diane, are you saying I'm trying to turn you on? I mean, because it's a known fact that I like white women so much."

"I think we should end this discussion right now," I said, feeling that he was teasing me a little too much. As far as I was concerned, he was dismissed, but it was obvious he didn't see it that way. He made no move to exit my car. I couldn't see pushing this young man away, especially when he smelled the erotic possibility of some white cunt.

"I've never been with a white woman," he repeated, as if he expected me to do something about that oversight, like I was part of some "field evidence" he wanted to gather. "Have you ever had a black man, Diane?"

Before I could answer, he kissed me so hard and fast my head spun and my panties became instantly wet.

With some reluctance, I managed to push him away. "I'm not conducting any research here," I let him know, trying hard to sound indignant. He had no right, asking me such a question and absolutely no right putting his lips on me. I pushed myself away from him. "I'm not about to serve you my cunt in the interest of research."

"Is that so?" he said as he moved toward me.

It was almost as if, in spite of my protest, he could see how much I wanted his cock buried inside me. I never had a black man, but everything he said and did made me want him more and more. Still, I didn't want to be considered "easy."

That's why when he came within striking distance, I slapped him hard across his smirking face. I surprised him, but it didn't stop him. He just grabbed my shoulders and kissed me again, this time thrusting his tongue between my lips. Soon I was moaning with my tongue dueling with his.

"Your place or mine?" he asked when he finally took his tongue out of my mouth.

I had to admit I wanted more.

"Your place," I said breathlessly, "but only because we're already here."

I'm giving my cunt to a black man, I thought while exiting my car. I walked a little ahead of him as we entered the apartment building. In the elevator, standing so close to his masculinity, I felt small at five-five and barely one hundred and ten pounds. As we rode up to the twenty-third floor, I couldn't help but wonder if he would like my 34-25-36 figure.

Inside his bachelor apartment, he flicked on the lights. The sparsely furnished living room had a fresh, clean soft pine scent permeating the air, as if he was expecting company that evening. However, I quickly replaced that thought with admiration; he was just a young man who kept a neat apartment.

Before following him into his bedroom, I kicked off my pumps in the living room. Once inside, I found it to also be neat and sparsely furnished. He went over to a mini-music entertainment center as I reached under my gown to pull down my sheer white pantyhose. When my legs were bare, I rolled up my pantyhose and put them atop his long dresser. Suddenly the bedroom was filled with the soothing sounds of Luther Vandross. I didn't know many R&B singers, but I knew Luther, thanks to you, Hillary.

Reaching out, he grabbed me and pulled me into his arms. I felt light as he moved my body in tune with the soft, romantic music. I really wanted to talk to him, let him know I wasn't some loose white woman, but that I was with him because the essence of his style and manner had captivated me.

There I was about to climb into his bed because everything felt so right. I didn't want him to think I was putting out just because he was a black man and I had *jungle fever*. However, I said none of this as we danced.

Because he had removed the jacket of his tux, I was able to run my hands up and down the front of his white silk tuxedo shirt. Still, that wasn't enough for me. I unbuttoned his shirtfront, then reached inside to massage his hot flesh. I opened his shirt wider, then bent to suck on his dark nipples. I moaned and groaned because as I teased him with my mouth, his big hands massaged my hot behind.

It was I who pushed him away, not able to stand anymore sweet torture of our foreplay. "Please," I begged, "let's take everything off."

It was almost like a race to see who would get naked first. I won and quickly climbed into his bed. I watched intently as he pushed down his boxer shorts. With him still standing I reached out for his stiff cock. Rubbing it between my hot palms, I was amazed at the rigid smoothness of it. As I took him into my mouth, he reached down to massage my cunt lips.

"So wet," he remarked as he stuck two fingers inside me.

He had me squirming all over the bed. I felt like the hot white woman of his dreams as he made me burn and cream for him, the flow from my cunt embarrassing as he shamelessly fondled me.

"I've got to have you inside me," I told him as I pulled him on top of me. When he pushed his big cock inside of me, I threw my legs up so they rested on his shoulders. I reached down to feel his cock as he ran in and out of me.

"Screw me! Screw me hard!" I screamed as I bounced my ass up and down on his bed.

The sight of his dark brown cock disappearing in my dusky pink cunt took me over the edge. I groaned as my cunt clenched and released over his hot stiffness. My legs trembled as I lost all control.

Then he grunted and came inside me.

"You're too much," I said while snuggling close to him, his naked body covered by a single sheet, my naked body too hot to be covered by anything. I just couldn't get enough of his hands on me, especially on my hot behind that had become one big erogenous zone, a creamy white behind I wanted him to fondle and lick.

My hand searched under the sheet until I found his magnificent cock, still thick, but soft now. He had shot a mighty load in me.

"I want you again," I told him. "I want you hard and inside me again."

"I have to rest a bit."

"I can get you hard again," I boldly told him, wanting him urgently inside of me. I trembled with my need for him. I whispered softly as I threw my bare leg across his thigh. "This hot, white woman wants you inside her so bad. So damn bad, baby."

"I want you, too. I really do," he replied as I moved to kneel between his wide spread legs.

"I'll tell you a story, a nice hot story to get you hard."

He laughed like there was no story I could tell that would get his cock hard for me.

"You asked me if I had ever had a black man," I said while holding his cock with one hand and tickling his balls with the other.

"And you never answered me."

"Does it matter?"

"I'm just curious."

"You want to know if I had another black man's cock inside me."

"Only if you want to tell me."

"You think I'd just let any man, black or white, screw me like this?"

"How would I know?"

"Would the thought of another black man being inside me turn you on?"

"I'm just curious, Diane. No big deal, really."

"You want to know if I sucked his cock like I sucked your cock? If I licked his balls like I licked your balls?"

"Only if you want to tell me."

"After the time we had, you know I'll tell you everything you want to know. I know I'll be sore tomorrow morning because of the way I indulged myself. Still, I want you stiff and big inside me."

"I don't think that's going to happen tonight, Diane. Perhaps in the morning before we leave."

"I want you now, and you *will* get real hard once I tell you my story, Professor."

"The story of you with another black man?"

"I've never been with another black man; you are my first. But I have been with a black woman."

That's when I told him about you, Hillary.

"A professor that once worked at the university," I began, my head resting on his chest, my hand wrapped around his cock. "We went to a conference in Greensboro, North Carolina, representing the university. I believe they sent us because she said we wouldn't have a problem sharing a room. I drew the line at sharing a bed, but the room was big with two queen beds. Since most of our time was taken up with seminars and symposiums, we had very little time for any sightseeing, but we did do some fun stuff, like shopping at the mall and seeing comedian Chris Rock in concert at War Memorial Auditorium.

"I had a ball and Professor Hillary Boston got to see another side of me, my backside. Or at least that's what she noticed when we got back to our hotel room. She told me how nice my backside looked in the dark blue tailored slacks I wore. She told me most white women she met had flat behinds and was somewhat surprised by the roundness of mine. I giggled, somewhat giddy from our drinks after the concert. I can't remember whose idea it was to compare behinds. Somehow, I don't think it was mine; I don't think I could ever be that bold.

"Hillary wore a short skirt and lifted it to show off what she called her 'big black ass.' But I didn't see it as too big or too black. She is a light-skinned black woman, and her behind was the color of coffee with a lot of creamer added. Because she wore a thong, her behind was fully exposed.

"Things got real crazy when Hillary suggested I remove my slacks so she could get a good look at my behind. Still giggling, and not believing what I was doing, I turned away and dropped my slacks to my ankles. But that wasn't enough for Hillary. She asked me to pull down my panties so she could see my entire behind. I posed for her, and even shook it a little in her face. At the time, I thought it was fair, considering she showed me all of her behind. I sat on my bed as Hillary removed her skirt and pulled down her thong. Bare like that, it looked even bigger and rounder, the cleft between her cheeks even deeper.

"As she stood there with her hands on her round hips, I shyly touched her behind. I guess you could blame it on the wine. I found it to be butter soft, and because she didn't seem freaked out by another woman touching her, I used both my hands. It was a good minute or so of behind rubbing before Hillary excused herself and went into the bathroom.

"I got real nervous because I thought I had gone too far. I was sitting on the bed, my behind still bare when Hillary came out of the bathroom. My first thought was to apologize for the liberties I had taken with her hot, ripe womanly body. But because she came out of the bathroom naked, I didn't feel there was anything to apologize for. She told me that I had gotten her wet. Then using two hands, she opened herself for me and showed how wet I had gotten her. She stood so close to me that I could smell her arousal.

"I reached out to touch between her thighs, and stroked her thick black bush while massaging my own wet cunt. She held onto my wrist as I shoved my fingers in and out of her hot wetness. I moaned loudly when her hands cupped my breasts. Her legs were spread wide as she removed my top and bra. When she fell on top of me, I fell back onto the bed and spread my legs wide, too. Her hands roamed from my neck, to my belly, to my cunt. Of course, I wanted more of her. Showing some athleticism, Hillary moved her long, thick body so that her hot behind was in my face and her face was between my thighs. We ate each other out until we screamed, trembled, and climaxed."

Needless to say, at the end of my story, the professor's cock was rock hard. And since I was so crazy with need, I gave him what I thought he expected from a white woman. Because I had given everything else, I felt there was only one last thing to give. I got down on all fours in the bed and let him know there was nothing I would deny him, my first black man. As he took me like that, all I could say was, "Your big cock feels so good in my ass."

I am writing this as I sit in my condo, alone. He called me this Monday morning after our great weekend, our unreal weekend. He called me from the university, concerned because I called in sick. I just couldn't get out of bed. I only wanted to lounge around and think about us. With no shame, I told him that I couldn't wait to see him again, that my body ached for him. He asked me if I had made up the story of being with a black woman. I laughed because only you and I know how very true that story is.

Being with him has made the memories of you and I even sweeter. It also brought back to my mind something you said as we were coming back on the plane from Greensboro. I didn't know how true those words were at that time. You said, and I quote, "Once you go black, you never go back."

Yours truly,
Diane